Gone Mia: Deadly Deception

TESS RAYNES

Contents

Chapter 1

The White Knight - Mia

According to the data, Mia's 2020 Toyota Camry should be the safest sedan she could have chosen. Yet, somehow, she's stranded on the side of the road, body wedged under the vehicle, trying to identify a "jacking point" so she can get on with trying to change the tire herself. Her phone is beside her head, caked with dust and sweat, and Sara's voice rings out.

"You have to make sure you find the right spot," she says, reading a how-to article on how to change your tire when it goes flat. "Or the vehicle could slide off the jack and crush you."

Mia screws her face up, pausing in placing the old rickety jack she found in her trunk. Cars are whizzing by on the highway, and each time, a gust of hot wind, dust, and gravel whooshes under the car, stinging her bare legs.

A rock is digging into her shoulder. Her blouse is definitely ruined from the sweat stains and dirt. Though it's barely May, it's already stiflingly hot.

"Maybe you should just wait for the tow truck," Sara says, worry laced through her voice. "I don't know if this is the best time to test out your roadside assistance skills."

"The tow truck is on a five-hour wait," Mia repeats, returning to her job of positioning the jack. "I'll die of dehydration before they find me."

"You're so dramatic. But also, I don't want you to die of dehydration. Or, like a cartoon character, crushed under your car."

"You're gonna be so proud of me when I do this; just wait. It's a step forward for woman-kind."

"For your information, I've changed a tire before. I could probably change a tire, even being pregnant. I think this is more about you than woman-kind as a whole."

"Semantics."

Mia tunes Sara's sarcastic response out and pulls the crank on the jack, hoping she's got it in the right position.

What's there to lose? If she messes up, she'll just be crushed and leave her poor parents to grieve the loss of their only daughter. She makes a mental note to check the statistics regarding car-jack-related fatalities if she makes it home.

"Hey, there."

With an embarrassing shriek, Mia jumps, hitting her head underneath the car. The pipe she hit lets out a low, metallic clang that harmonizes with her groan of pain.

"What was that?" Sara asks, her voice low and serious.

"Someone's here," Mia hisses, eyes shut against the pain.

"Oh shit," someone says, leaning down to look at her as she slides out from under the vehicle. Crouching there, next to her car, is a ridiculously handsome man. He pushes his hand into his dark hair, sweeping it back out of his eyes. "I'm sorry," he says, offering her a hand so she can right herself. Mia ignores it and pulls herself up to sit, her hand against the throbbing spot on her temple.

"I'm sorry," he says again, glancing between the tire and her. "I didn't mean to spook you. I just thought you might need a little help."

Mia peers at him, squinting through the blazing mid-afternoon sun. What is the statistical likelihood that this man is a serial murderer seeking out stranded women on the road? Mia knows from crime documentaries that you're more likely to trust beautiful people, and that's why so many serial killers are handsome.

"I'm doing just fine," Mia says, drawing her hand away from her face and looking at it. She sighs with relief when it comes back dusty—but blood-free.

"I can see that," he says, quirking an eyebrow. His gaze flits past her and to her tire, which looks like it went through a cheese grater. The tread hangs down from the rim like long pieces of black spaghetti. "Holy shit," he says, shifting and running a thumb over one of the shreds. "You're lucky this didn't damage your wheel well."

Mia shifts uncomfortably, still unsure how on-guard she should be. Her phone is still slightly under the car and still on the line with Sara, who knows enough to stay quiet. Pregnant Sara may not be the best audience for her violent murder, but at least if this man turns out to be homicidal, there'll be a witness to the crime.

"What do you mean?" Mia finally asks, her curiosity getting the better of her.

"This kind of force, from the blow," the man says, gesturing to the tire. "I've seen tires like this cause a lot of damage." He turns and glances up and down the highway. "You're also lucky you didn't swerve into someone, or off the road."

"Yeah," Mia says, resisting the urge to roll her eyes. "I'm feeling very lucky right now."

Her tires are less than a year old, and she maintains her car with almost fanatical care. How the tire ended up like this is beyond her, and also beyond frustrating.

The man is standing, circling around her car, a hand to his chin, like he's trying to find the secret spot of damage. Mia struggles to her feet, starting to get annoyed at his interruption. She just needs to get her spare tire on and get home.

"Oh," he says, pointing to her rear windshield. "The Reid Walruses! Did you go to school there?"

A hot flush crawls up Mia's cheeks, and she almost wants to reach out and cover the sticker with her hand. She can picture Sara on the other end of the line, covering her mouth to stifle her giggle.

When she earned her associate degree from the local community college, her dad insisted on getting matching bumper stickers featuring the school's mascot. And now, this has invited a strange man into further conversation with her.

"Yeah," she hears herself saying, the word broken in the middle. She clears her throat. "I did a year and a half, got my associate degree and a certificate in data analytics."

He raises his eyebrows, looking her up and down again as though re-appraising her.

"I love that place. I took some welding classes, mechanics stuff there. The instructor was very cool."

Mia holds her hand up against the sun, looking this man in the face again. Despite herself, she doesn't actually feel that awkward talking to him. It's not like she's incapable of social interaction, she just prefers other communication. Like email or texting—something where she can edit and refine before sending. When she's forced to talk in person, it feels too immediate. Too vulnerable.

"I'm Alex," he says, drawing her out of her thoughts. He holds out his hand, and Mia considers it for a moment before taking it reluctantly. Her hands are dirty, but feel small in his grip, like how she felt holding her dad's hand as a little girl. His fingers are callused, rough, and something about that sends a thrill through her.

"Mia."

"So, Mia," he continues, "I'm actually a mechanic. Worked as a tire tech for a few years. I can get this swapped out for you in no time, no crushing necessary."

"I don't know," she says, remembering where she is. On the side of the road with a strange man, no way of escaping.

"Please," Alex says, and his earnest tone makes Mia pause. "It's like how a doctor might stop to help with an emergency. This is like my civic duty."

Mia lets out a surprised laugh, meeting the smile in his eyes.

"Your civic duty, huh?"

"Yes, and I would be very pleased if I could help you get back on the road."

"Okay," Mia says after hesitating for a moment. "Okay, Alex the Mechanic. Please, show me how to change this tire."

"Don't worry about that," he says, his eyes crinkling. He fishes something out of his pocket and holds it out to her. "Here, why don't you sit in my truck, cool down? Go on to the driver's seat. I trust you not to take off with it."

Mia closes her fingers around the keys. She wants to protest, but sitting in the driver's seat must be safe, right? And she can't deny that sitting in the air conditioning for a few minutes sounds amazing.

She mumbles a thank you and walks to his truck. She takes a quick picture of his license plate with her phone, which reminds her that she's still on with Sara. She makes a mental note to check for data on how many serial killers own a white 2015 Chevy Silverado. After a second, she realizes that's probably too specific and revises to consider how many serial killers own trucks.

It's so big she has to hoist herself inside, but once she's in the driver's seat, with the A/C blasting, she finally feels herself starting to relax. Alex is moving quickly, and Mia realizes he brought his own jack, one that you don't have to crank, and he's placing it confidently under the car. Her eyes wander over his strong back, how it curves when he reaches under the car, how capable he looks as he lifts the car, grabs the spare tire.

"Hello, Earth to Mia?" Sara's voice whispers from the phone, still on speaker. "What's going on? Someone came to your rescue?"

"Yes," Mia says, not taking her eyes off Alex. She balances her phone on her thigh. "Alex the Mechanic."

"Is Alex the Mechanic hot?" Sara asks, barely keeping the squeal out of her voice. Even though Sara is married

"You're so weird," Mia says with a laugh, trying to ignore the way her cheeks flare. If Sara was here right now, she would have no problem clocking Mia's attraction.

"Oh, Mia, you think he's hot, don't you? You should ask him out!"

"No, Sara," Mia says, pressing the backs of her hands to her cheeks. "He's just helping me change my tire."

"I'm just saying, it's been a while, hasn't it?"

"I'm hanging up."

"Don't hang up! You're in mortal danger! With Alex the Mechanic."

Mia hangs up the phone, the mortification of the situation almost too much. She takes a deep breath. Alex is kneeling, the spare tire next to him on the gravel. Not wanting him to look back and catch her watching, Mia closes her eyes for just a moment. If this is what it feels like to let someone take care of her for a moment, she could see herself getting used to it.

***

A soft tapping to her left rouses Mia from sleep, and she looks around groggily, not remembering where she is. The sun, once glaring through the windshield, is starting to set along the horizon, washing the sky in violet and pinks.

Her stomach growls loudly, and she tries to remember the last time she ate. She had breakfast with her mother this morning. What time is it now? She smells leather, rubs her hands over her eyes, and looks over to the sound to find Alex standing outside his truck, gently tapping his fingernail against the window.

Realization hits her: she's locked him out of his own truck and fallen asleep inside. Her cheeks are cool from the A/C, but they warm again as she quickly twists the key in the ignition and unlocks the door, feeling her clumsy limbs flail as she jumps down to the ground. She has that distinct feeling of stepping out into the heat when your body is cool to the touch.

"I'm sorry," she says, at the same time he says, "Good nap?"

She puts her head in her hands as he laughs good-naturedly. The world feels so soft and far away, and she wonders whether it's from her short sleep or from his presence.

"Hey," he says, and she feels a jolt as his hand brushes against the back of hers. "Don't worry about it. Anyone can see you've had a rough day."

The way he's talking to her, looking at her, the brush against her hand   maybe Sara was right. Maybe it has been too long.

Mia nods and looks back at her car, which now has one tiny tire in place of the regular one. She'll have to take it to a tire place tomorrow, but right now, all she wants is something to eat. Her stomach growls loudly again, and it makes him laugh.

"I don't know how I can thank you enough," she says, "but I should probably get going. Really, thank you, I don't know how long I would have been waiting on a tow truck if you hadn't come along."

"You know," he says, "there's a diner just up the road. Buddy of mine runs it, the burgers are excellent."

At the thought of a burger and fries, her mouth starts to water.

"A buddy of yours?"

"Yeah, name's Dave. He's a part-time fry cook, part-time private detective, so I can offer you dinner and some juicy gossip from around town," Alex says, raising his eyebrows suggestively.

"I don't know," Mia says, glancing back at the car.

"Tire shops are closed by now anyway," Alex adds, holding his hands up, his face softening as he looks at her. Mia feels almost like he has a certain gravitational pull, like she couldn't walk away from him if she wanted to. And maybe she doesn't want to.

He was kind enough to stop when he saw her stranded on the side of the road. What harm could come from grabbing a burger with him? Mia imagines what Sara would say: "How you can expect to find the right man if you don't give anyone a chance?"

"Okay," Mia says, finally, "but I'll pay. As a thank you."

"Whatever you say," he says, smiling. He follows her, going forty miles per hour, to the diner, to make sure she makes it okay on the donut. Inside, he orders a chocolate milkshake and offers to share it with her, then sneakily goes to the bathroom and pays the bill before she even has a chance to get her wallet from her purse.

Later, standing outside the diner, he leans against the wall, one hand over her head and says, "I'd like to see you again."

Mia looks at Alex, considering. When she was stranded on the side of the road, dating was the last thing on her mind. Now, her eyes running over his strong jaw, her body reacting to his presence, she's changed her mind.

"I think we can make that happen," Mia says, boldly reaching up, grabbing him by the collar of his shirt, and pulling him in for a kiss.

Chapter 2

Settling In - Mia

ia wakes up slowly, feeling the empty bed beside her, reaching out for where Alex should be. Hearing sounds from the kitchen, she sits up and stretches. Her back pops and her collar bones loosen, and she catches sight of herself in the mirror. Her cheeks are flushed, her eyes bright.

Alex has been sleeping over at her place nearly every night, and when he's not at hers, she's at his. A month has passed since that day she was stranded on the side of the road, and they've seen each other basically every day.

Mia knows that, statistically, people are more likely to be optimistic in the morning, but she can't help thinking about what it would be like to live with him.

It's still too early in the relationship for that—and Alex may not even be interested—but she can't stop thinking about what it would be like not to have to run back to her own place for clothes or watch him leave extra early for work.

In the bathroom, he has a dark blue toothbrush next to hers, and his Old Spice deodorant sits on the counter next to a travel bottle of his cologne. She glances at the door, then, quickly, brings the cologne to her nose, taking a quick sniff. She loves the smell of it, wishes she could keep a bottle of it on her desk.

Mia brushes her teeth quickly, and as she's spitting in the sink, her phone starts to buzz.

"Good morning, darling," her father says, and she moves to sit on the edge of the bed, tapping her fingers against her knee.

"Morning, Dad. What's up?"

"Oh, I just wanted to give you a little update on your mom."

Mia tenses, immediately expecting the worst. Every time she gets a call from her dad, there's a chance it's bad news. She still remembers that first, terrible call. Diagnosis. Dementia.

Mia tells herself that her dad wouldn't have such a light tone if something truly bad had happened.

"Nothing bad," he says, as though sensing her apprehension. "Actually, it's quite good. We heard back from that experimental drug trial, and your mother was accepted."

"Oh, that's great," Mia says, trying to sound chipper, though the previous two drugs hadn't helped, and had only made her mother's grogginess worse.

"She starts next week, and I was hoping you might be able to take her to her appointment."

Mia's father was always doing this—assuming that because she worked from home, she could handle all the errands. She'd tried to tell him that she still needed to be available for calls and questions, but he didn't understand. Putting her dad on speaker phone, she multi-tasked by requesting a partial day off while staying on the line with her dad.

"Speaking of Mom," Mia says, clearing her throat and trying to ease some of her nervousness. She's never introduced someone to her parents before. "I was wondering what you think about introducing her to someone?"

"What do you mean?" her father returns, clearly puzzled.

"Well, it's not, like, super serious or anything, but I'm seeing someone, and I was thinking it might be nice to introduce him to you guys."

"Oh, honey," he says, and Mia feels like she should be offended at how surprised he is. "That's great! I think as long as we pick a familiar place and make sure we catch her on a good day, she'll have a great time. But you might want to warn him that she may not remember him. If we see him again."

Mia's chest pinches. It's not super serious, like she said, but there's some part of her that wonders if Alex is the one. It feels like all her friends are off living their own lives, and after meeting Alex, Mia is starting to see the appeal. Despite herself, she thinks about her mother at the wedding, greeting Alex as though meeting him for the first time, and Mia has to press her lips together to keep from tearing up.

They move on to lighter subjects, chatting about their upcoming trip to see a Braves game at Truist Park. When she was younger, she just wasn't interested in baseball. Her dad begged her to come to a game, tried to talk to her about the team, but she was too busy burying her head in her books, preparing for an upcoming Mathlete competition.

Then, one summer, she walked into her dad's study while he had a sports show on, and they were talking about stats. He'd come wandering in minutes later with a fresh coffee and found her sitting there in her pajamas, transfixed. Since then, they'd found a crossover for their hobbies: she liked to geek out over the baseball data, and he found someone to sit next to at games. For a while, they'd had season tickets, but when her mom got sick, they reduced their attendance to just once per season, usually in September so it could coincide with her dad's birthday.

After discussing the latest player trade, Mia tells her dad she loves him and gets off the phone. For a moment, she stares down at the birth control pills in her hand, trying to remember if she's taken them. The packet is supposed to help her track, but she must have forgotten to change the sticker so the days line up correctly. Wanting to err on the side of caution, she pops a pill from the packet and takes it quickly.

Still wearing Alex's shirt from the night before, she pads down the stairs to the kitchen, where Alex is finishing up the dishes. He's in nothing but a pair of red flannel pajama pants slung low on his hips, focusing on a plate in his hand. It's sexy when he cleans, and she leans against the doorway, watching.

He has the kind of torso that's soft but strong, with refined muscles you can tell come from manual labor, and not hours spent at the gym. Mia thinks about the night before, and how he'd picked her up so easily when they tumbled into her bedroom.

He's nothing like the other men she's been with. He's capable. He puts the toilet seat down. He does his own laundry. Mia makes a mental note to review the data about men who know how to do laundry.

"Babe," he'd said the week before, tapping on her furnace one day. "When was the last time you replaced this filter?"

"I do it every month," she'd called back from her office, where she was cleaning up a set of data. A headache was humming low in the back of her brain. Alex had brought her a Diet Coke, and she was nursing it, hoping it would ease the thrum of pain.

"I see," he'd said, appearing in the doorway to her office. He was wiping his hands on his jeans, gazing at her, and for a moment she hoped he'd be proud of her for taking good care of the house, but instead, he furrowed his brow. "Did you clean around the filter?"

"What?"

"You have to clean around the filter, too. Otherwise, the build-up there causes problems."

"Oh," Mia said, mortified to feel a lump in her throat. She was going to cry over this? Her boyfriend giving her home maintenance advice?

"It's okay, baby," Alex said, and Mia felt even more embarrassed that her emotions were so clear to him. She turned her head, covering her eyes with her elbow. Then she felt Alex over her, bending down so he could kiss the side of her neck. She hated feeling the tears pushing behind her eyes.

"It's okay," Alex said again, "You didn't know."

"I'll do it this weekend when I have some time," Mia said, "I'm just really swamped with this project, and the project manager keeps asking me for updates—"

"Don't worry about it, babe," Alex said, straightening up and taking her face in his hands. "I'll do it."

"No, Alex, I know it's my responsibility—"

"Let me take care of you, okay? I know you're stressed. I'll take this off your plate."

Mia feels a swell of gratitude rise up in her, remembering him down on his hands and knees, cleaning around the furnace. She'd sat next to him, pushed him over, and crawled right into his lap.

Now, the floor creaks beneath her feet and Alex turns, his face lighting up when he sees her. He's so handsome like this, and Mia lets her eyes drift over the patch of hair on his chest, the intricate tattoo circling his forearm.

"Good morning," he says, quickly setting the dish on the rack and crossing the kitchen to her. His arm goes around her, his palm on the small of her back, pulling her flush against him for a smoldering kiss. That's one thing Mia has learned quickly about him—he doesn't do quick pecks. Even when they're leaving a restaurant, or she's greeting him at the car, he does the whole thing, or no kiss at all.

Mia melts into it, trying to think of the last time she was this infatuated with a guy. None of her other boyfriends were like this, so clearly into her. Sara would argue that Mia hadn't given them a chance. In Alex's arms, smelling whatever he has in the oven, she promises herself she won't block him out like she's done with other guys.

Alex pulls away, breathing hard, but keeps his hand on her lower back. Slowly, he ushers her over to the breakfast bar, nuzzling against her neck as he gently pushes her down into a seat.

"Let me make you some coffee," he says, pulling away.

"Oh," Mia says, already pushing her hands against the counter to get up and make it herself. She's very particular about the ratio of milk to sugar to coffee, but Alex puts a firm hand on her shoulder.

"Please, Mia," he says, his hand tightening for just a moment. "Let me take care of you."

That, coupled with the slow, melting Southern drawl, sends a rippling wave of lust through her, and she bites her lip as she watches him cross the kitchen, grabbing coffee beans and the grinder.

"I've been thinking," she says, looking down at her lap, where she's tracing a circle on her thigh. These moments with Alex, early in the morning before she starts to get pings from work, and before he has to go out, are the best parts of her day. "I know we haven't been together very long, but I'd like—well, I was wondering if you might be interested in meeting my parents."

Alex looks up at her, pausing with his hand on her mug, and for a second Mia's afraid she's pushed too far, asked for too much. Then, a slow grin spreads over his face, and he's in front of her, pushing the coffee her way.

"You really want me to meet your parents?" he asks, a vulnerable note in his voice. Mia takes a careful first sip—it's a little too bitter for her taste, and probably needs more sugar, but Alex made it for her, so she won't complain. She feels a quick tightening in her chest at the look on his face, so eager.

"Yes, of course," she says, setting the mug down again. "I understand if you think it's way too early, but—"

"If you want me to meet them," Alex says, putting a finger under her chin and lifting her face so her eyes meet his, "then I want to meet them."

***

"Is that what you're going to wear?"

Mia jumps, putting her hand to her mouth as Alex appears in her bedroom, sidling up behind her in the floor-length mirror. She's trying to learn not to startle so easily.

For the dinner with her parents, she's wearing a simple blouse tucked into black trousers, with the matching pearl earrings and necklace she got from her mother. Mia had been going for elegant but understated, but now she turns back, re-evaluating the look.

"I don't know," she says, though she had coordinated her make-up and hair around this outfit.

Alex smiles carefully, and Mia turns around to look at him. He looks like he's trying to decide what to say. He's wearing a simple button-up with gray pants, and his hair is a little neater than normal. Mia resists the urge to reach up and tousle it so it falls in his eyes.

"What? You don't like it?" she asks, trying to ignore the way her body reacts in his presence.

"You look beautiful no matter what you wear, you know that, but I thought this place was... fancy."

Mia presses her lips together, looking down at her bare feet. Her father had suggested the nicest Italian place a town over, where he and Mia's mother had been celebrating their anniversary for years. It was as familiar as they could get in public. She thinks about countless celebrations there: her high school graduation, associate degree, getting a promotion.

"Here, love, I got you this," Alex says, pulling Mia out of her reverie. She looks up at him, seeing a white, rectangular box in his hand. She can't help smiling as she takes it from him.

Gift-giving must be Alex's love language, because he's always offering her something—a better pair of headphones, perfume that isn't too strong, a new comforter for her bed that's more breathable.

Mia opens the box to find a sparkling gold dress, but as she pulls it out and holds it under her chin, something about it doesn't feel right. She lowers it, comparing it to her current outfit.

"It's a little... nicer," Alex says, running his hands over her hips and holding the dress up under her neck, so it covers her blouse again. She can tell the dress is going to be tight, and she'll need to wear Spanx and pantyhose with it. "It'll look so good on you, babe," he continues, moving her hair to the side and kissing her neck. "I can't wait to peel it off you later."

Mia's melting back into him, his hands heating her body, and for a moment, she thinks about putting off the dinner with her parents and just staying home. But no—she hasn't seen them since breakfast with her mom before her tire blew. And besides, she wants them to meet Alex.

She steps away, rolling her eyes playfully at him.

"Don't get me all worked up," she says, then dances out of his reach and to the bathroom. "I'm just going to change into this quick, then we can go."

***

They're ten minutes late to the restaurant, and Mia can tell Alex is in a sour mood. She keeps tugging on the hem of her dress, willing it to be longer, wishing it wasn't so skintight. It took her some time to adjust her make-up and find a pair of shoes nice enough to wear with the dress, and by the time she was ready, Alex was sitting on the bench by the door, tapping his foot.

The valet is full and they have to park down the street. Alex whips his truck angrily into a parking spot, nearly hitting the car next to them. He stalks down the sidewalk and Mia struggles to keep up with him, hobbling a bit in her heels.

Her parents are already seated when they arrive, her father looking up sharply when they come in. Mia has always thought her parents were good-looking people, but now, every time she sees them, she's shocked at how old they look.

Her father's face is lined with wrinkles, his salt and pepper hair thinner than it once was. Mia's mother used to chide him, saying he was lucky to keep his hair at all, as most of the other men in his family went bald long before sixty.

Mia's mother's hair was still long and dark, braided elegantly down her back. On one of her bad days, Mia had found her sitting in front of the mirror, where she had been brushing her hair for over an hour, forgetting how she normally styled it.

The Italian place is dark and mood-lit, with soft orchestral music playing from hidden speakers. It's the kind of restaurant where the servers all wear formal attire and real plants are nestled in the shelves and on the walls. The air is thick with garlic and butter, and Mia's mouth waters as she leads them to the table.

Alex's face is carefully blank as he pulls the chair out for her, and she wishes she'd been able to get ready faster. She'd be frustrated with him if he had made them late to meet his parents. Mia longs to lean over and put a hand on his face, help him calm down, but once he sits down, he's out of her reach.

She settles with running her foot along his leg, and to her relief, he doesn't pull away, glancing over at her and giving her a small smile. She opens her mouth to introduce him, but the waiter appears to take their drink orders.

"I'll have the Merlot, please," Mia says, sharing a conspiratorial glance with her dad, who is a firm believer in white wines only. It's a constant debate in their family.

"And for you?" the server says, looking to Alex, who stares down at the menu for a moment longer, then glances at Mia, raising his eyebrows.

"Red wine will stain your teeth, love, maybe you should go with the Riseling."

"Oh," Mia says, as the waiter looks back to her, pen poised over the pad in his hand. He looks bored, annoyed that she's changing her order. "Yes, you're right. The Riesling sounds wonderful."

Alex smiles and pats her hand on the table, then orders a water. He's driving home, and Mia glances at her parents, as though to say: See? He's responsible.

But Mia's dad is frowning at Alex over the top of his wine menu. He doesn't even look away when he orders a glass of Pinot Grigio for himself and a seltzer for Mia's mom.

As soon as the waiter is gone, Mia leans forward, giddy at the thought of finally introducing Alex to them. She feels the dress pull against her bust and quickly yanks it back up, wishing the neckline was just a bit higher.

"Mom, Dad, this is Alex. Alex, my dad, Drew, and my mom, Charlotte."

"It's so wonderful to meet you," Charlotte says, and Mia notices that particular light behind her eyes that means she's here, and not somewhere inside her head. "Mia hasn't introduced us to one of her boys before, so you must be special."

Mia blushes, hard, and tries to glare at her mom without the others seeing, but Charlotte is oblivious to the hard look. Her dad and Alex exchange greetings and the waiter returns, delivering drinks and pouring wine. Mia notes her dad's pinched brow as he takes a sip of his wine.

"So, Alex," Drew says, setting his glass down and placing both hands on the table. "Are you a Braves fan?"

"Oh," Alex says, laughing a bit, "no, I'm not really into baseball. More of a football kind of guy."

"I'm sure Mia will convert you," Drew says, raising his eyebrows and taking another sip of his wine. "I'm honestly surprised she hasn't yet."

"Oh, we don't really talk about sports," Mia says, fiddling with her napkin and hoping to move the conversation along. When she'd mentioned her interest in baseball stats, Alex had kissed her distractedly on the temple and changed the subject. So he wasn't into baseball—lots of people enjoyed other sports more.

"What do you do, Alex?" Charlotte says, and Mia could hug her for the convenient change in topic.

"I'm a mechanic by trade," Alex says, tapping his fingers gently along the outside of his water glass, "but my real passion is creating metal sculptures. I'll get scrap metal from work and make it into something new."

"They're gorgeous," Mia says, pulling her phone from the black leather clutch she brought, since this dress was sans-pockets. She clicks to the gallery app, intending to show her parents one of the sculptures.

"Oh," Alex says tersely, putting his hand out and pushing her phone down. At the feeling of his large, warm hand on hers, she clicks the screen off, feeling her face heat. "We don't need to bore them with pictures."

"Reduce, reuse, recycle," Charlotte says, grinning, as Mia nods, forces a smile, and tucks her phone back into her clutch.

Charlotte raises her glass and Alex gamely clinks his against hers. "I always wanted to be an art teacher," Charlotte continues, "but I just didn't have the artistic chops."

"You could always get back into it," Alex leans forward, bracing his elbows on the table, and Mia cringes. Her father is weird about table manners, and she can almost feel Alex losing points with him. "You could come around the shop someday, I could show you some of what I do."

"You know, the Caddy could use an oil change," Mia's dad says, gesturing with his glass. She hates how he refers to their Cadillac as "the Caddy" making it more casual that they own a nicer car. Mia wants to save face with Alex, add that it's the same SUV they had when she was a kid, but the moment passes.

"Come to my shop," Alex says, grinning broadly, but Mia notices a slight tick in his jaw. "I'll get you a discount."

After their food comes, the night passes quickly, and Mia is grateful for the opportunity to bury herself in eating her seafood alfredo, dunking the garlic bread in the sauce and savoring the blend of flavors. It reminds her of a celebration, and she glances around the table as they eat, catching her mom's smiling face and how her dad enjoys his beef tenderloin. They're a family of habit—ordering what they know is good.

Mia is standing in the foyer, waiting for Alex to pull the car around, trying to wedge her lipstick back into her tiny clutch when she smells her dad's familiar cologne.

"Oh," she says, still struggling with the bag. "Hey."

"Mia," he says, and at the tone in his voice, she looks up at him, her hand with the lipstick going still. "I'm glad you brought Alex to meet us, but…"

He's cut off as Alex pulls up with the car, eyeing Mia expectantly. Her dad holds up a hand for a moment, gesturing for Alex to give them a moment. Shifting his body, her dad blocks Mia's view of the truck and Alex, lowering his voice conspiratorially.

"Mia, I'm just concerned that Alex seems a little pushy."

"I think he was just nervous, Dad," Mia says, laughing and trying to glance around her dad so she can get a glimpse of Alex to make sure he isn't frustrated at having to wait.

"You don't like white wine. And frankly, I've never seen you wear a dress like this before in your life."

Her eyes snap to his, defensive. She's never really argued with her dad, but right now, she feels a new type of anger bubbling up.

"He's thoughtful, Dad. That's what happened with the wine, and I'm just branching out, trying a new style. Alex is honestly the best thing that's happened to me."

"Honey," her dad says, putting a hand on her shoulder gently. "He seems a little egotistical. I'm just worried that—""Almost ready to go, honey?" Mia jumps and her dad's hand falls from her shoulder, Alex's hand replacing it a moment later. When her dad narrows his eyes at the touch, she quickly raises her hand to Alex's, throwing him a smile over her shoulder.

"Yeah, sorry, just finishing up," she says.

Her dad frowns again, his gaze lingering on Alex's hand, but he doesn't finish his thought. Instead, he steps forward, pulling Mia to him and giving her a firm hug.

"I love you, honey," he says.

"I love you, too, Dad," she says, as Alex waves to Drew, takes Mia's hand, and pulls her to his idling truck.

Chapter 3

Time to Break Free - Mia

"**I** have a surprise for you."

Mia blinks slowly, feeling Alex's warm breath on her cheek. When she turns, his face, warm and soft, is so close to hers that she can't help but reach up and give him a kiss. He turns his face, gesturing for her to sit up.

Once her back is against the bedframe, he sets a white rectangular box on her lap.

"Go on, open it up," he says, and she giddily pulls the tape from the sides, revealing a navy and white striped bikini.

"Oh, Alex," she says, holding up the two-piece in front of her. She thinks of the simple black one-piece suits she typically chooses and tells herself that this is a fun improvement. "This is so cute."

"I'm glad you like it," he says, rolling out of bed. Mia watches his calves flex as he stands up in a pair of board shorts, grinning down at her. "Because you'll get to use it today. Get up, get dressed, I've already got the truck packed."

"Oh," Mia says, shaking her head and lowering the suit down so it pools on the tissue paper in the box. "Alex, I can't today. I have work, and—"

"Don't worry about that," he says, coming to her side of the bed and taking her wrists in his hands. "I've thought about it already—you can just call in sick. It's not like they'll ever know."

"But I've never called in sick before."

"Exactly, so they have no reason to think it's not true."

"But I feel bad about lying—"

"Fuck, Mia, you can just say you don't want to go to the beach with me."

Alex reaches out, taking the bikini in his hands, and Mia feels a surge of panic go through her, so she grips it tightly, pulling it back.

"No, I'm sorry, I just—I'm still a little sleepy. I want to go to the beach with you, Alex, that sounds so fun. I'll call in sick, just this once."

"No, if you don't want to go, I'll just return the suit." His voice has turned completely sour, and he still has an iron grip on the swimsuit. Mia tightens her hold, feeling the slippery-smooth fabric under her fingers.

"Please, Alex, I'm sorry, I wasn't thinking clearly. I'd love to go to the beach. Please."

He looks at her for a long moment, his chestnut eyes stern and flat, having completely lost the twinkle they had just moments ago, when he woke her up. A lump forms in her throat, the panic making her skin tingle. She feels stupid for being so ungrateful when he planned this for her—none of her other boyfriends had planned dates, or gotten her clothes.

"Fine," he says, voice apathetic, before he turns and walks out of the room.

Rushing, Mia runs to the bathroom, pulling on the swim suit. It's a little snug on her, but it's flattering that Alex thinks she's this small. She'd much rather wear a one-piece, but with her tantrum already this morning, she thinks she'll just compromise and wear the suit he got her.

In five minutes, she's brushed her teeth, thrown on a sundress, and tied her hair into a braid. She's running down the steps when she hears Alex's truck start up in the driveway, so she hurries faster, unable to shake the feeling that he might leave without her. Hastily, she grabs sunscreen and a towel from the closet, stuffing them into a tote bag. Her flip flops smack noisily against her feet as she runs to the passenger side, leaping up and trying to ignore Alex's steely glare out the windshield as she buckles her seat belt.

He's clearly upset, revving the engine and braking hard, and after ten minutes passes, Mia slowly sets her hand on his thigh. Alex glances over at her, still wearing that flat look, and she gives him a small smile.

"I think it's going to be a good day," she says, infusing her voice with positive energy. "Look at the sky, those clouds."

Alex glances up through the windshield, at the huge rolling clouds above them. It's a perfect day for the beach, Mia realizes, feeling even more silly for her breakdown.

"Yeah," Alex says, and a moment later, Mia feels his hand cover hers. Though they do sometimes get into fights like this, Mia likes how Alex is always quick to forgive her and move on. She'd once dated a guy who would linger on every miscommunication, drawing the arguments out for days.

Mia settles back in the seat, watching the scenery roll by and feeling lucky.

***

The beach is crowded with families and tourists, and it's clear that everyone else was equally inspired by the weather. Alex, somehow, manages to find a space for their cooler and towels, setting up their area quickly and scooping Mia up, running with her into the water.

She keeps covering her stomach with her hands, feeling exposed in the bikini, but Alex loves it, running his hand under the ties on the sides and in the back. While they're in the water, he grips her thighs and nuzzles into her neck, and she looks around, nervous that parents might berate them for PDA.

Fortunately, Alex gets hungry and they head back to their cooler. He assembles cold chicken tacos with guac and cotija, and Mia drips them all over herself, which Alex claims is reason enough to get back in the water.

After another round of splashing and playing, they're back on their towels, and Mia closes her eyes against the sun so when she opens them again everything's washed in blue. To her right, she feels Alex repositioning, propping himself up on his arm, looking down at her.

She laces her hands over her stomach, squints against the glare of the sun to see his face.

"What?" she laughs, finally, "Why are you looking at me like that?"

"Mia," he says, reaching out and tucking away a loose piece of hair. "I wanted to talk to you about something."

Her heart picks up, but she tries to act nonchalant. Is he going to ask her to move in with him?

"It's just that… you've been kind of down lately. Since that night we went to eat with your parents. That's kind of why I wanted to take this trip, to cheer you up."

"Oh," she says, fiddling with the tie on her bikini and trying not to look at him. She lets her head fall back into her towel, feeling the sand give way to her weight beneath it. "I'm okay, really, it's just…"

She thinks about her mom, who had lost her light immediately after the dinner, soiling herself on the ride home and forgetting her dad, so he'd had to pull over until she calmed down and fell asleep. Her dad had called to tell her about it the next day, and brought Alex up again, how he didn't like his behavior that night.

Mia hadn't meant for the conversation to get heated, but she'd found herself raising her voice.

"For Christ's sake, Dad, the first guy I ever introduce you to, and you can't even give him a chance?"

"I gave him a chance, Mia, at the dinner. And I didn't like what I saw. He was too controlling. If... if your mother could discuss it with me, I'm sure she'd feel the same way."

"It is so not fair to bring Mom into this."

"Do you really think your mother would be okay with a man treating you like that?"

"Treating me like what? Driving me there? Driving me home? Pulling out my chair? Buying me a new dress?"

"Alex picked out that dress? I knew it wasn't something you would wear on your own. Don't you see that, honey? You seemed like a different person."

"I should be allowed to change. I don't have to stay the same all the time."

"You're absolutely right, but it should be you doing the changing, not your boyfriend."

Mia, for the first time in her life, hung up on her dad, and they hadn't spoken since then. Now, she feels tears behind her eyes, threatening to spill over if she doesn't reign them in. She wishes, more than anything, that she could get her mom's opinion on Alex, but she can't.

"...things have been a little tough," Mia finishes, lamely.

"I know your dad doesn't like me."

Mia jolts up, sand rolling off her shoulders, and turns to look at Alex sharply, examining his face for signs of anger.

"It's not that," she says quickly, waving her hand, "it's just that—"

"I'm not mad," Alex says, chuckling at her distress and grabbing her hand, quickly bringing it to his lips. His mouth is hot on her cold hand, and it makes her shiver. "It's clear your parents have a lot going on," he continues, "and maybe they're not ready for you to not be with them all the time. I'd probably be nervous, too, if I were your dad. Especially with what your mom is going through."

Mia feels a tear slip down her cheek, warm and salty against her skin. A breeze ruffles her hair and she closes her eyes, tipping her face to the sun. Despite only knowing her for a short time, and only meeting her family once, Alex read them like a book.

"It's been the worst," Mia finally says, not looking at him. "My mom was my best friend. I talked to her about everything. She was my rock, and now, when she looks at me, she doesn't know who I am."

Alex tugs on her hand, pulling her back down to the blanket and tucking her head under his chin. For the first time in a long time, she allows herself to cry, ignoring the fact that other beach-goers can see them, ignoring how this position might look like PDA. She allows herself the space to grieve her mother while she's in Alex's arms.

When she's finished crying, Alex pulls her back and wipes her face with his t-shirt. They stay there like that, together on the sand, for a long moment, then Alex speaks, his voice low, rumbling against her.

"Maybe you should give them some space."

"What?" Mia's voice sounds rough, foreign to her own ears. She pulls away from Alex's chest and looks into his face. His eyes are bright, focused, meeting hers solidly.

"I just think... if you give them some space, take some space for yourself, maybe your dad can get over his fear of change. We can work on our relationship, and after we've had some time we can show them we're the real deal."

"You think we're the real deal?"

"I know we are," he says, kissing the tip of her nose. A long silence passes again, in which Mia feels so full of contentment, happiness, staring up at the puffed clouds above her, that she forgets what they were talking about.

"So, what do you think?" Alex asks, breaking the silence again. The sun is starting to set, and they're some of the only people left on the beach. Mia watches the sky as it descends into brilliant colors, her mind feeling slow, hot.

"I... I'll think about it."

Alex seems to accept this, pulling her closer and running his hand over her thigh absently as the sky darkens around them.

***

Mia's standing outside the shower, fishing around in her bag for her t-shirt, when her phone starts to buzz. She turns, reaching into her purse to grab it before it rings out.

"Hello?" she answers. Her entire body feels heavy, slow. A whole day of swimming and sitting in the sun does that to you.

"Mia!" Sara's voice comes through the phone. "You never called!"

"Never called?"

"You said you would after the meeting with your parents. Remember? I wanted to hear about how it went. With Alex."

"Oh," Mia rubs her hand over her forehead. "That's right—I completely forgot."

"That's okay," Sara laughs. "I mean, it took me a whole week to call you. I've been busy, too. But I just got out of a gyno appointment, and it popped back in my head."

Mia pauses, knowing she should ask about the appointment to make sure everything's okay with the baby, but she finds it hard to focus suddenly.

"So?" Sara asks, interrupting the silence after a long, quiet moment passes.

"So..." Mia feels the happiness from the day seeping away, and she rolls her shoulders. "So, it didn't go great, actually."

"Oh, no," Sara says, knowing in her voice, "your mom?"

"No, not exactly," Mia rubs her hand over the back of her neck, checking her watch. She wonders if Alex is waiting for her at the truck. "It's just my dad; I think he's not ready for me to be with someone."

"What?" Sara's voice is light, confused.

"Like, with everything going on with my mom. I think I'm going to take some time away from them."

"Time away from... your parents?"

"Yeah, I think—Alex, well, it's probably for the best."

"Did Alex tell you to do that? To stop talking to your parents?"

"Not stop talking to them. Just, like, give them some time to adjust. My dad has his hands full with my mom, and I don't think he's ready for me to have something else to occupy my time. I think Alex and I need to focus on our relationship without that distraction."

"The distraction of your parents?" Sara's voice is agitated now. "Is Alex—"

"It's not Alex," Mia snaps, switching the phone to her other ear. "It's both of us, making the decision together. It's what's best."

"You should just talk to your dad about this, Mia. From what I know about him, it's hard to believe he'd unfairly judge someone like that. I wish I could come over and chat. I hate that I'm so far away from you now—"

"You're the one who made the decision to move." Mia's shocked the moment it comes out of her mouth. She doesn't feel in control of her own body, just wants this conversation to end.

There's a hurt moment of silence.

"You know I wanted a better school district for the kids," Sara says, softly. "But that doesn't mean I don't care about you. It just seems like Alex is asking you to do a lot of big things so early in your relationship."

"You haven't even met him!"

"But from what you're saying, and the way you're acting—"

"You and Ben may have issues, but that doesn't mean everyone's relationship is fucked." Mia puts her hand to her mouth, eyes wide at her own statement.

Sara is quiet for a long time, and Mia realizes she can hear her own breathing loud, bouncing off the shower wall. Her heart is hammering. She wants to fight, feels like she's been holding back, holding it all in, and she's not sure where it came from.

"Okay," Sara says in her mom voice, "that was hurtful, Mia. Why don't you call me back when you're ready to talk."

"Sure."

"Fine, okay."

Mia hangs up without saying good-bye, her body buzzing with anger and pent-up energy. As she quickly towels off her feet and throws her shirt on over her suit, her brain supplies her with lines she could have used, clever things that would have changed Sara's mind.

As soon as she sees Alex waiting outside, leaning against the truck, she decides that she'll call Sara back another day. Or maybe plan for them to meet each other. If Sara met Alex in person, she'd understand.

Mia pushes the thoughts from her mind as Alex grins at her, giving her a kiss before he opens the truck door and helps her hop in.

Chapter 4

Trust Issues - Alex

Alex can tell that Mia loves her house. Though she's renting, her landlord welcomes tenant improvements, so Alex's first visit was a show-and-tell of each improvement she'd made. The fancy bronze faucet in the kitchen, the ash gray cabinets, the new tiles on the floor. In her room, she had one of those four-poster beds from every teen movie, colorful floral wallpaper. It was nauseatingly feminine, but Alex dealt.

Now, Mia is sitting in her office, puzzling over a spreadsheet she can't seem to figure out. Alex stands just out of sight in the hallway, watching her drop her head into her hands. He's never been a math guy, remembers hating solving problems in class with a vengeance, being asked to the board, where he'd stand dumbly, unsure of where to even start. It was humiliating.

He may not be good at math—may not be as smart as Mia, but there is something he's good at, and that's people. Frank, at the shop, is Alex's favorite to get in the bar and hustle. He's fighting with his pregnant wife and wants to stay out playing pool all night, even if that means handing over hundreds to Alex every night.

Alicia, one of Alex's previous girlfriends, had been so obsessed with how she looked that a single side glance at her outfit would send her into spirals. It was exhausting, but simple. If he wanted her off his back, he'd suggest she find something better to wear.

Mia, though, she's different. He hadn't realized it on the side of the road, talking to her for the first time, but she's one of the brightest people he's met, with an automatic suspicion that must have come from someone betraying her trust in the past. It became clear that her mind was her best asset. It was also clear that she relished having someone take care of her, and Alex got the feeling that someone hadn't done it well in a long time.

Alex watches her drop her head to her desk and slips down the hallway silently, back to the kitchen, where he's making lunch. He chops strawberries and walnuts and adds them to a dark green salad, then sets a dark chocolate pudding and tops it with a single cherry. When he returns to Mia's office with the lunch, she pulls her head up from the desk quickly. She doesn't want him to see her struggling.

Alex sets the food down, running a hand over her hair, which is soft and warm. He sets the food down and slides it between her and her keyboard.

"You gotta eat something, baby," he says, nudging the food toward her again.

She glances down at it, then quickly back at her computer screen.

"This project," she says, tears clearly in her eyes. "It's due tomorrow, and I just— it's like the numbers are swimming. I can't get my head to latch on to a single thing. I've never felt like this before."

"Here," Alex says, dragging a chair up and sitting next to her. He pushes the salad away and grabs the pudding. "Start with dessert. That will make you feel better."

When she doesn't move, he grabs the spoon and scoops some pudding, holding it up to her lips. She glances at him, laughing a bit at him feeding her, then opens her mouth obediently. It sends a thrill through Alex, and he watches her tongue and lips and she licks the pudding from the spoon.

"It's good," she says, after swallowing. "Kind of... bitter."

"It's dark chocolate," he says, tapping the side of his head with his free hand. "Brain food. I thought you might need it."

She lets out a watery laugh, propping her hands under her chin and accepting another bite.

"So," Alex says, when the pudding is gone. He pushes the salad toward her and gestures for her to eat. After she takes a bite, he continues, "I heard you talking to your dad this morning."

"Oh," Mia says, color flooding her face. "I'm sorry, I—"

"You don't have to apologize," Alex says, leaning forward and wiping a tear from her cheek. "I know how it is. That's your dad, but it kind of seemed like a... tough conversation."

Tough was one word—Alex had heard Mia practically yelling at her father, defending Alex's honor. He'd stood outside the door and listened as she told her dad Alex was good and kind and honest and he'd felt a particular kind of tug in his heart.

"Yeah," Mia says, dragging her fork through the leaves but not bringing more to her mouth. Alex watches, but doesn't intervene. It won't matter if she doesn't finish the salad.

"Well, I was thinking," he rubs his hand along the top of her thigh under her desk, and watches as she turns, leaning into the touch. "I just wondered if those kinds of conversations are affecting your mental state. Making it hard to concentrate on your work."

She seems to think for a moment, then drops the fork into the bowl.

"I think you're right," she says, "it's just so hard because... he's my dad. I just don't understand why he's acting like this."

"Parents are weird," he says, widening his touch, pressing his whole hand to her thigh, noting how big his hand is compared to her leg, touching the tip of her knee and where her leggings bunched at the hips. "My dad, he was kind of like that."

Mia's head snaps up so fast, Alex has to press his lips together tightly. It's clear that she's been waiting for him to share something like this, something deep. But sharing is hard. He likes to keep his cards close to his chest, usually, but right now he goes on.

"My dad left me—left us—when I was just a kid. Didn't even get to see my first steps. My mom struggled. Nobody should have to raise a baby on their own."

Mia puts her hand over her heart, nodding softly along as he speaks.

"Obviously, growing up without a dad sucked, but it taught me a lot," he looks up into her eyes, letting out a little bit of that hurt his dad left behind. "Taught me what not to do, that no matter how hard things can get in a family, the worst thing you can do is to leave. Give up. Quit. Once I have my family, I'll never, ever give up on it. But I'll also never suffocate my kids. I want them to be their own people, you know?"

Mia rubs her hands over her eyes to try and disguise the fact that she's crying. Alex looks away, allowing her to compose herself. After a few shaky breaths, she finds her voice.

"You know," she says, drumming her fingers on the desk. "Talking to my dad has only made me more upset. I think—I think you're right. I think I need to take a break from talking to them. At least until he can come around and stop trying to control my life."

Alex places his hand on her back, rubbing softly, then pulls her into him sideways, giving her a tight hug.

"Sometimes letting go is the hardest—and best—thing you can do

Chapter 5:

Confusion - Mia

Mia jolts, hearing a loud alarm. After a moment, she realizes it's the fire alarm, and the egg in her pan is black, torched and smoking.

"Shit," she says, grabbing the pan and tossing it in the sink, running it over with cold water. She tries to find the step ladder so she can get up to the smoke alarm, but it's not in the closet. Instead, she drags a chair over and stands on it, reaching on her tip toes to press the button. The alarm doesn't stop.

Reaching up, her shirt riding up her stomach, she grabs the edges and tries to twist the alarm, to take the batteries out, but it won't budge. Grumbling to herself, she gets off the chair and grabs the broom, jamming it up against the alarm, harder and harder, trying to turn it off, shocking herself when it busts and pieces of plastic come raining down on her, one hitting her in the eye.

"Fuck." She drops the broom and tips her head, her eyes immediately watering from the pain. And then her eyes are still watering, and she's sitting on the floor, clutching her knees to her chest, heaving with sobs.

For a fleeting moment, she wishes Alex were here. He would comfort her, make her breakfast, fix the smoke alarm. She wouldn't have to get up and face what she's done, clean up the mess, stare at the blackened eggs.

Lately, it feels like her head doesn't belong to her, like she's constantly reaching out for thoughts as they slip through her fingers. She's never felt like this before, and starts to wonder if she should see a doctor.

When her legs and back start to go numb from sitting on the floor, she pulls herself to her feet and tries to salvage the situation. First, shaky because she hasn't eaten, she pulls a protein drink from the fridge and nurses it at the table. Once that's done, she follows it with a glass of water and feels marginally better.

She reaches into the sink and collects the waterlogged, blackened egg, dumping it in the trash. Once the pan is washed and dried, she puts it back in the cabinet. There's not much she can do about the smoke alarm—it's in a million tiny pieces across the floor. She sweeps up the plastic debris and adds new smoke alarm to her grocery list.

Once the kitchen is looking relatively normal, her heart slows down and her brain feels more in reach. Then, a moment later, the lights flicker off.

"For fuck's sake," she mutters, finding her way to the garage. Luckily, it's daytime, so the light coming in through the windows keeps her from tripping and landing on the floor again, but when she reaches the garage, her anxiety and frustration has skyrocketed. Can something not go wrong, for once?

She finds the breaker box and confidently switches the primary power switch back and forth. This has happened a few times, when she tried to run her hair dryer at the same time as her microwave, and a quick reset was all the system needed.

Now, though, nothing happens. She runs the switch again and to her dismay, the house stays dark. When she goes back through the door, she can already feel it starting to warm up in the kitchen, growing muggy. The warm air combines with the smokey smell and makes her slightly nauseous, but she persists.

"Hello?" she says, when the representative at the energy company answers the phone. "I think you might need to send someone out. All my lights are out."

After collecting her name and account number, the representative gives an awkward cough.

"I'm sorry, Ms. Agostini, it seems we've had to temporarily suspend your service, as the bill hasn't been paid in more than two months. If we can go ahead and run a payment now, we can get that turned right back on for you."

Mia feels a cold sweat break out on the back of her neck. Two months? She'd never missed a single payment in her life, let alone for two consecutive months. She fumbles with her phone, asking the representative to give her a moment.

When she opens her online banking account, she sees that it's far, far too low. Where's her money? She checks her savings account, which is also low. There are tons of charges for fast food, restaurants, random purchases, and she puts a hand to her mouth as her memory comes back to her.

Yes, she remembers buying these things, but why hadn't she checked her account? She always used to be so vigilant about her balance and keeping her savings account up. And now her savings is in the double-digits, her checking account also shockingly low. When was the last time she even logged into the app?

"Ms. Agostini?" came the voice on the other end of the line. "Are you there?"

"Yes, sorry," she says, clearing her throat. "I'm sorry, I just... I'll call you back."

"Would you be interested in completing a short—"

Mia ends the call, feeling guilty about cutting her off mid-sentence, but she can't stand the thought of staying on the line for a moment longer.

"Something is wrong with me," she whispers into the empty room, feeling eerily like someone is watching her.She rubs her sweaty palms on her jeans, and in the same moment, feels her phone vibrate in her pocket. It's her manager asking for an update.

Before the egg incident, Mia had been prepared to go upstairs and put together the project update. Now she's forgotten completely about it and feels too scrambled.

Her phone buzzes again. Panicked, she takes the steps two at a time and just manages to accept the call from her manager, Brandy. Mia's still breathing hard when her video connects and shows her disheveled, still in her pajamas, and wiping the sweat off her forehead. On her desk, her phone battery turns red, depleting quickly from the hotspot she's enabled to replace her wi-fi.

"Mia," Brandy says, raising an eyebrow. "If this is a bad time, we can reschedule."

Brandy's tone is so full of implications—it shouldn't be a bad time, it's during working hours, after all, during the time Mia is expected to be ready for meetings and other communication.

"No, no," she says, struggling to regain her bearings. "This is a fine time. Sorry for the delay, let me just..."

Mia trails off, clicking through folders, trying to find the data she's been compiling. Suddenly, she can't remember how her organizational system works. It's like she's sifting through someone else's computer, desperately trying to unearth a file she's never seen before.

"Hey, Mia," Brandy says, her voice surprisingly empathetic, "why don't you regroup, and we'll meet tomorrow, first thing in the morning? With that update ready to go. How does that sound?"

Mia lets her head fall, adrenaline and embarrassment coursing through her body, only just tinged with relief at Brandy's words.

"Yes, that sounds great; sorry, I just—this has been kind of a hectic morning."

"It happens to the best of us," Brandy says, tucking her shiny blonde hair behind her ear. "We'll reset and restart tomorrow."

"That's perfect, thank you so—" Mia cuts out in the middle of her sentence, left staring at the NO CONNECTION screen on her laptop, her phone lying dead beside her on the desk.

For a moment, Mia just stares at it, then she pushes her chair back and drops her head into her hands. In the quiet of the room, she can feel her head spinning slightly like she has vertigo. She closes her eyes, thinking she'll just rest for a moment, and when she wakes up later, Alex is rousing her, bringing her dinner to her desk.

Chapter 6

The Humiliation and the Shame - Mia

The faint smell of smoke is still tangible in the air when Mia wakes up the next morning, cuddled firmly into Alex's warm body. A rush of affection goes through her at the thought of him, and she remembers how he'd come over last night with a new smoke alarm. He got in touch with the energy company and got the lights back on—Mia had promised to pay him back, but he'd held his hand up, not even entertaining the idea.

Now, Mia slips out from under his arm, stretching and reaching for her phone on the bedside table. Weirdly, it's not plugged in like she thought and comes away freely. In the next moment, she realizes the screen is staying black, no matter how many times she taps at it.

"Alex," she says, suddenly wide awake. If her alarm didn't wake her up, then what did? She sees the bright sun coming in under the windows. What time is it?

"Alex," she says again, nudging him and watching as he lolls awake.

"Hey, love, what's wrong?"

"What time is it?"

"What?"

"The time, Alex, can I check your phone? What time is it?"

Mia leaps out of bed and makes to reach for his phone, but he's already picked it up, rubbing his eyes and looking at the time.

"It's about ten," he says, sitting up and giving her a quizzical glance. "What's the matter?"

"It's ten? It can't be ten. Oh, no. No, no, no. My phone went dead!"

Mia's already an hour late to the meeting with her manager. The second meeting, the restart, rescheduled meeting Brandy had been kind enough to offer her. Mia runs to her office, powering on her laptop, and landing in the chair, hard. When it finally comes to life, she has two missed video calls and a series of chats from her manager, asking her where she is.

A chill of dread shakes Mia's body as she reads the last message.

Brandy Heloux: Let me know when you're on, Mia. We need to talk.

By the time Alex comes into her office with a cup of coffee, Mia has already messaged Brandy multiple times, apologizing profusely, scheduling another meeting, and sending the update Brandy asked for. It's not perfect, but it's the best Mia can do. Her manager isn't available to meet until the next day, and Mia knows she won't relax until that's over.

"What's the matter, Mia?" Alex asks, setting the coffee down and kissing the top of her head. Mia twists around, falling halfway out of her chair and into his arms.

"I'm so stupid," she says into his shirt.

"Shh," he says, rubbing his hand up and down her back. "What's going on?"

"I'm so, so stupid. I didn't plug my phone in last night, and now I've missed this meeting, and it just feels like everything's going wrong."

"Oh, baby," Alex murmurs, still soothing her. "Everyone goes through rough patches. Your manager will understand. You just have to push through."

"I just—I can't believe I did that. I can't believe I've made so many mistakes."

"You'll get through this," Alex says, kneeling down and taking her head in his hands. "I know you will."

Mia closes her eyes and lets her forehead fall against his.

"I don't even know why you'd want to be with me. I'm a loser."

"You know what?" Alex says, tapping his finger against her temple. "I know what's going to cheer you up. Let's get lunch today, just me and you. I need to grab a new jacket for a thing with Dave. Work hard this morning, make some progress on your project, and then meet me downtown. We can try that new salad place."

Mia raises her head and sniffles, trying to keep the tears at bay.

"You know you love salads," Alex says dorkily, smiling at her, and Mia can't help the smile that breaks across her own face.

"I know what you're thinking," he whispers, moving his thumbs up and down rhythmically under her ears. "What's the statistical likelihood that a salad will improve your mood? It's 100%, baby."

"Alex," Mia laughs, feeling her lips move against his as she speaks, "that's not how statistics work."

***

Mia steps out of the door and stops, lifting her face to the sun. She closes her eyes and breathes deeply, catching the scent of the roses she planted just outside the door to her house. Despite her lack of care recently, they've been thriving. She makes a mental note to prune them this weekend.

She's missed being outside. Her mind seems clearer, but that strange fuzziness lingers.

In town, she keeps her head down, not wanting to speak with anyone, but her eyes dart around, searching. Her parents are unlikely to be out, though. She knows her mother hates crowds and finds the shops confusing.

The shops downtown are bustling with people, and Mia stops in a little boutique to buy a scarf from the window before heading to a more formal clothing store down the street.

Mia finds Alex in the menswear section holding up a linen jacket, which would go beautifully with his eyes. For a moment, she hangs back, looking at him and feeling some joy flood back into her body. Everything else might be going wrong—whatever's been faltering in her brain—but she has him.

"Hi," she says, loving how he turns, an infectious smile taking over his face when he sees her. She stands back and folds her arms like she's the judge on a fashion show. "That one looks just right."

"Hi." He leans over and presses his lips to hers, pulling her body against his for a long moment. When they break apart, she glances around, hoping a shopkeeper didn't catch their long embrace. Luckily, nobody's around. She catches a waft of Alex's usual aftershave, which makes her smile.

"You think?" Alex says, pulling back and holding the jacket up again.

"Sure. Sexy but understated. And that gray really suits you."

He shrugs it on, and she smooths out the shoulders, feeling the firm strength of the muscles under her fingers. The grin he gives her makes her melt.

"That was easy, then," he says, laughing. "Could you put these ones back while I pay? Then we'll grab a couple of salads."

Mia puts down her purse and takes the pile of discarded jackets to the rack, fitting them all on. Alex holds out her purse when she returns. "Here, don't lose this. I've got to run—I just got a call about a stalled car on North Road." He gazes into her eyes. "You okay to get home alone?"

"Of course. I just need to pick up some lunch before I head back to my desk."

She watches him leave. Lunch together would have been nice, but if she can get home quickly, she can work on that issue Mark had flagged on her last project. She's thinking better today, so she might be able to see the solution. Mia is still deep in thought as she walks out onto the street.

Moments later, a patrol car pulls up alongside her, lights flashing. She stops, confused, looking around to see who they want. No one else seems to be around. She frowns as the policeman climbs out of his car slowly, then lumbers over, hitching up his belt.

"All right. Let's not make a fuss. Why don't you give me a look in that bag?"

Mia smiles, even as static rushes through her ears. That same anxiety that's been plaguing her all week returns, covering her body in pins and needles. "What's the problem, officer?"

"We've got a report of shoplifting, so if you don't mind..." He points lazily at her purse like he has all day to hold her up.

Her cheeks flush as people stop to watch. The crowd behind her is older; their judging stares are so much worse than if it had been a couple of teenagers. "Sure. There's nothing there," she says confidently, already trying to look forward to the moment the cop apologizes for wasting her time.

Mia opens the bag, and he peers inside, his meaty hand moving aside her scarf.

"What's this then?"

She gasps. Inside, still in the packaging with a security tag attached, is a brand-new iPhone. The plastic wrapping glints in the sun as the cop raises it out of the bag, saying something into his walkie-talkie that she can't make out through the roaring in her head.

"That's not mine," she gasps. "I've no idea how that got there."

Hearing a woman murmur behind her, she whips around. There are three elderly women, one of which Mia recognizes. Susan, from her parents' church, who brings the scotcharoos, and is delighted at Mia's decision to join the choir in high school. Susan narrows her eyes at the stolen item, then at Mia. She purses her lips and taps the woman next to her.

"Mia!" Susan says, putting her hand over her heart as though the scene is just too much for her. "What will your mother think?"

Mia feels ice creep down her spine and wants to lunge forward; tell Susan not to say anything. They'll surely get everything worked out.

"Miss," the cop says, his hand closing around her upper bicep. "You're going to need to come with me."

***

"I'm so embarrassed," Mia says, her voice heavily muffled by Alex's chest. They're in bed together, but Mia's been able to do nothing but cry.

"Things have been hard for you," Alex says, pulling some of her hair away from her neck. After the cop had taken her back to the station, she'd felt like a real criminal. They took her fingerprints, read her rights, and gave her a date for court. It was high on the list of the worst things that had ever happened to her, and she could only hope the information didn't get back to her mother.

What was even more humiliating was the fact that someone at the station had called her dad, who showed up, shock and anger on his face. After he paid her bail, they were walking out of the station together, and Mia surprised herself by breaking the silence first. They hadn't spoken since she hung up on him during their last conversation.

"You're not going to tell Mom, are you?" she heard herself asking.

"What? No, of course not," he said, looking baffled. "It's not... it's not worth upsetting her."

Another moment of silence stretched as they neared the parking lot.

"What in the world is going on with you, Mia?" her dad asked, his hands buried deep in his pockets. He was wearing a pale pink collared shirt and ironed shorts—his golfing clothes.

Mia stopped short, not wanting to delve back into the conversation. He'd turned toward her as though he sensed she wasn't beside him still. When their eyes met, Mia felt the strong urge to cry, step into her dad's arms, and explain everything that was happening to her.

But she didn't do that because it was impossible to explain, and for a fleeting moment, she worried that she'd gotten the dementia gene from her mom, only hers was coming on much sooner. And it was better to never talk to her father again than force him to go through that twice.

"Nothing's going on with me. I told them I didn't take that phone. Why would I take the phone? I have my own!"

"Mia," her dad said carefully, "John, down at the power company, gave me a call—"

"What?" Mia felt her eyes widen. Her dad actually thought she was capable of stealing? Why would it even make sense for her to shoplift where she lived? If she was going to resort to stealing, she knew she would be a lot smarter about it. But the worst part of all of this was that now her dad knew about her struggle with the bills, which no doubt helped to explain why she might try to steal and sell a phone. "How—how—that's a violation of my privacy! They had no right to call you!"

"Please," her dad said, taking another step toward her, his hands still up, palms forward like she was robbing him. For some reason, the note of pity in his voice made her even angrier. "Just talk to me. Maybe—maybe it's time for you to come home. Your mom could use the company, and—"

"This conversation is over," Mia said, turning on her heel and ignoring her father as he called after her. It was a long walk home, but it had given her time to think and time for her to get more than thirty notifications. Someone had posted a video of her encounter with the cop, and the hate comments flooded in.

Now, even though she's set her profiles to private, her phone continues to buzz on the side table. Mia closes her eyes. Maybe her dad was right—maybe she does need help, but she's certainly not locking herself away in her childhood bedroom.

"Alex," she says, twisting around in his arms and finding his eyes, trying to hold back her tears. "I know—I know this is kind of soon, but how would you feel about moving in together?"

Chapter 7:

Refuge - Alex

Alex's mother had a bad case of shingles nearly a year ago. During that time, her face was scaly and red, her temper on edge, an angry expression hidden by her collection of floral silk scarves. She refused to be seen in public until it wore off. The downside of that experience was Alex's near-constant vigilance of her mood swings, the cocktail of medicine that barely did anything to help, and Alex's fear that he might catch it from her.

The major upside of Blanche's encounter with shingles is the leftover prescription of Gabapentin she got for nerve pain but never actually took. With over three bottles of the stuff, it's been too easy for Alex to slip it into Mia's lunches and drinks, and despite claiming to have a great palate, Mia had never seemed to notice anything wrong.

Now, standing in his mother's kitchen, Alex tips the bottle up and reads the side.

Side Effects: Drowsiness, dizziness, nausea, diarrhea, headaches, memory loss. Do not take with alcohol. Do not operate heavy machinery while taking this medication.

"Oh, honey," Alex's mother is saying when he returns to the room with a tray of hot drinks. Blanche sits across from Mia at Blanche's kitchen table, her wrinkled hand covering Mia's. Mia looks, as she almost always does lately, very close to tears.

"Thank you, dear," Blanche says when Alex delivers the tea. He's very careful to set the cup with the slight chip in front of Mia, who blows on it for a second before bringing it to her lips. "As I was saying," Blanche continues, as Alex takes a seat at the table with them, "this actually happens to a lot of women nearing your age. Are you on birth control?"

Mia blushes and glances over at Alex, who raises his eyebrows at her. It's not something they've discussed, but he'd assumed she would be on birth control. She didn't seem like she was particularly eager or ready to have a baby.

"Yeah," Mia says, glancing back at Blanche, who's tapping her rings gently along the side of her cup. Alex wants to tell her to stop but won't risk the backlash. "I started shortly after..."

"Oh," Blanche says, waving her hand in front of her face, grinning conspiratorially at Mia, "you don't have to spell it out for me, dear. But something to consider is how birth control can affect your body. Doctors try to tout that stuff like it's harmless, but I had a girlfriend who took it and, a few months later—a stroke. Apparently it came out of nowhere, but that birth control was known to raise blood pressure. And she had been having terrible headaches."

"Oh no," Mia says, tightening her hands around her cup. "I never... I didn't know there were such severe side effects. I mean, I guess they do list them on the medication, but it never feels like they'll actually happen."

"Yes, well," Blanche says, taking another sip of her tea and glancing at Alex over the rim. "That might be something worth considering."

***

"Your mother is lovely," Mia says, grabbing her pillow and fluffing it up. Despite the many sets of lingerie and silk pajamas he's purchased her, she's still in a ratty t-shirt and pair of plaid pajama pants. He stares at her for a moment, feeling a wave of revulsion. Why can't she do the simplest things, like wear the nice things he's gone out of his way to buy her?

For the past few months, he's been stealthily using her bank account, getting cash back on simple purchases, changing her password to make it more difficult to log in, and intercepting her paper bank slips so she wouldn't notice her dwindling balances. It was too easy for him to intercept the rent check to keep the landlord from cashing it and to take down the LATE RENT notice he'd posted a few days later.

"That's nice of you to say," he says, trying to control the anger seeping into his voice.

"She was so... I mean, I guess it just felt like she wasn't judging me, you know? It feels like, with everyone else, Sara and Dad—it just feels like they aren't listening to me. It was nice how your mom jumped right into trying to help me solve the problem. I already feel so much better than I did a few days ago."

Luckily, Mia had a monthly lease on her house, and since she was already two months behind on her rent, her landlord loved the idea of her moving somewhere else, especially since she left behind all her improvements to the place. Alex would not miss the ugly four-poster bed or the annoyingly cloying roses outside the front door.

Mia mumbles something about going to the bathroom, and Alex slips into the bed, letting his body settle. It had been a long day at the shop, dealing with prissy car owners who didn't understand how to change their oil, let alone diagnose complex engine problems. And yet, every time he told someone their transmission was out or their alternator was failing, they never hesitated to come back with sarcasm or condescension, implying that he didn't know how to do his job.

Mia returns from the bathroom, drawing Alex out of his thoughts. He looks up to see her standing there in a set of skimpy silk pajamas. She has her arms crossed over her chest and is clearly cold, but he feels something inside him wake up, warming.

Lifting the blanket, he gestures for her to join him in the bed, and she climbs in happily, nuzzling into him. As he lifts her hair up and kisses her neck, undoing the top button of her pajamas, he thinks back to how his mother had been at dinner.

She'd insisted that they join her for dinner on Mia's first night in the apartment building, and they'd walked the flight of stairs up to Blanche's apartment, Mia toting along the lemon meringue pie she'd picked up from a bakery down the street. Blanche was overly kind, welcoming Mia in and making her feel like family.

Alex thinks of how the two of them had whispered while he was in the kitchen, serving their plates and making his tea. He doesn't like to feel like a servant.

"Alex," Mia whispers softly, and he wraps his fingers in her hair, tugging a little too hard.

He hadn't expected his mother to talk about Mia's birth control right in front of him—it was the kind of thing she usually insisted was "girls only" or "not conversation for the dinner table." It had made him a little uncomfortable, but it was a great cover for the side effects of the crushed drugs in Mia's food.

Dropping that iPhone in her purse had been easy. Unplugging her phone had been easy. Watching her get more confused and emotional had been satisfying.

And now that he has her here, in his apartment, in his bed every night, it's going to be even easier to finish what he's started.

Chapter 8

Sacked - Mia

"Good morning, Mia," says Brandy, her ever-polished face coming into view. There's something in her expression Mia doesn't like, like pity mixed with admonishment. Mia just needs to win Brandy over to show she's still valuable to the team. Since moving in with Alex, it's been hard to find a new routine, but Mia is determined. She will not lose this job.

She's momentarily distracted by another comment pinging on her social media. Only skanks steal what they can't afford.

"Good morning," she says, smiling brightly, trying to push through the sour feeling from the latest message. She hasn't stopped receiving them since the video of her and the cop went viral, and more people seem to see it as it acks up views. Every day, she checks to see if there are any positive comments or anyone defending her, but it's just a slew of criticism.

Mia silences her notifications and refocuses on the computer in front of her. She's wearing a blazer, as though she can remedy the last few disastrous meetings by over-dressing. "Let me just pull up my slides—"

Mia stops when the video chat dings, indicating that someone else has joined the chat. She clicks back to the window and feels her stomach drop when a man from HR is staring back at her.

"Oh," Mia says; at the same time, Brandy says, "Thanks, but we won't need those slides, Mia."

"Good morning," the HR man says, sharing his screen and pulling up a document titled Employee Termination.

Mia grips the chair beneath her to keep from passing out. Her head feels light, her heart flipping and dancing in her chest as though attempting to beat inside out.

"We're just going to run through some standard procedures, Mia. I'm sorry to say that your supervisors have reviewed your last performance assessment and determined you're not fit for your position. As of this moment, you are no longer an employee with the firm."

"But I'm the best data analyst you have."

"You are very qualified, Mia, that's true. And you have worked on some important projects. We're more than willing to give you a great recommendation letter, but you're no longer fit for this team. Your attendance, collaboration—"

"Collaboration? I've covered my team members countless times! I basically completed Mark's entire report last quarter!"

"That was last quarter," Brandy says cooly. "And now, we can hardly count on you to finish your own work."

Mia's body fluctuates between ice and uncomfortable warmth. She squeezes her hands together in her lap.

"I'm just going through a bit of a rough patch. I'll pull through, I'm just—"

"There's also the matter of your recent... criminal activity," the HR man says matter-of-factly.

Mia rears back as though he managed to hit her through the screen.

"What?"

How could they even find out about that? Mia thinks of her dad and wonders if he even knows enough to contact her employer. If he would do something like that, to try and get her home.

"It came to our attention that you're facing charges for shoplifting. As you can see clearly in our handbook, we require that our employees follow standard moral codes. In section 13(b), you'll see the clause about criminal activity. The firm is completely within its bounds to terminate you and deny unemployment, but because of Ms. Heloux and her insistence, we've agreed to offer you a severance package, which is much more generous than the situation warrants."

Mia's sobbing into her hands the second the call disconnects. Her email pings with the severance letter. She has one day to review and sign it. Her access to her documents, to everything she's done with the company, and to the chat program is immediately revoked. She feels empty.

After a long moment of hiccupping sobs and trying to catch her breath, Mia turns slowly in her chair, facing the inside of the room.

Because Alex doesn't have a second bedroom, she's set her home office up across from the bed. She stares at the pillow, still indented from where he was this morning. She wishes she could crawl into bed with him, let him hold her.

One part of her brain tells her to get back on her laptop and immediately start applying for new jobs, but her body doesn't move. Instead, she listens to the part of her brain that's insisting she find someone to comfort her.

A moment later, Mia's standing outside apartment 412, knocking on Blanche's door.

***

If someone had told Mia a few months ago that she'd be sitting on a floral print couch, getting a hug from a woman she barely knew, doused in the heavy scent of patchouli, she wouldn't have believed them.

"It's their loss, I promise. I'm sure you can find an even better position now that you have all this experience," Blanche says, pulling away from Mia's hug and reaching to the coffee table to grab her cup of coffee.

"It was just so sudden," Mia says, taking another sip from her mug. She usually tries not to drink coffee after lunch, but this feels like an exception. "I know I've been making some mistakes lately, but I didn't expect them to fire me just like that. I loved this job. Without it, it just feels like I'm aimless. I have no purpose."

"I'm sure there must be some other reason. Perhaps they were planning on doing lay-offs anyway, and you just happened to be an easy target."

"Yeah," Mia says, holding her mug with two hands and trying to let the steam comfort her. "The other thing is... well, you know about what happened at the store. I guess they found out about that? I'm not sure how, unless—I mean, I can't believe he would do something like that, but my dad might have called them. I just don't know how else they could find out."

"That is strange," Blanche says, absently running a hand over her neck, and Mia notices that for her age, her skin is surprisingly taut. She wants to ask if she's had any work done but gets the feeling that she's not the kind of woman who's public with her beauty maintenance. "Do you have a good relationship with your father, Mia?"

Mia looks down at her lap and realizes she's been wearing the same leggings for days on end. There's something—yogurt?—smeared across her thigh. It looks terrible, and she feels her cheeks warm. Next to Blanche, who's so prim and well-dressed, Mia feels like the wreck that she is on the inside.

Blanche is one of the most beautiful older women Mia has seen, with elegant gray hair she manages to make look intentional, always styled and pinned up perfectly. Though it's clear from her voice and her mannerisms that she's older, Blanche doesn't look old—even her hands are fairly wrinkle-free, and it makes Mia wonder if she's been adamant about applying sunscreen since the day she was born.

"Dear?" Blanche says, lowering her head and looking up into Mia's eyes.

"Oh," Mia says, rolling her lips, trying to remember what Blanche said.

"Have you been rather forgetful lately?" Blanche asks, worry creasing her brow.

"I... I guess, yeah," Mia admits, "but it feels like more than that. Sometimes it feels like my brain doesn't belong to me. If that makes sense."

"Oh, dear," Blanche winces, her gaze going far-off, like she's turning inward for a moment. "Right after I had Alex, I had a terrible time. Depression, made me feel like I was watching a movie of myself. Perhaps what you need is to see a professional about it."

"I've been thinking of that," Mia says, nodding, then laughing ruefully, "but now I don't have health insurance."

Blanche offers her a consoling look, and the room falls into another silence as Mia traces the rim of her coffee cup. Suddenly, Mia gets an intense wave of longing for her own mother. It's kind of Blanche to be here for her, to offer her comfort, but with her own mother, there wouldn't be awkward silences.

"I was just wondering about your father," Blanche finally says, very softly, as though she's scared she might frighten Mia away. "I know dads can be tricky. Alex's father was... not the easiest man to live with. He really hurt us when he decided to leave, and still continues making choices that aren't in his son's best interest."

"That must be so hard," Mia says, and despite everything, she feels grateful for her dad, who stuck around, at the very least. "My relationship with my dad has been complicated lately. We used to get along, but since my mom got sick, it's like he doesn't want me to change or grow. When I started dating Alex, my dad hated it. And Alex was the first guy I introduced to my parents."

"My," Blanche says, laughing a bit to herself as she leans back into the couch, "I can't imagine anyone not liking Alex! Though I suppose I'm biased."

Mia smiles for the first time all day, and the room gets quiet.

"I don't know how I would be making it through all this without him. I can't imagine coming into someone's life when it's at their hardest and deciding to stay."

"Alex is a good man," Blanche says, nodding and finishing her last sip of coffee. "He's never failed to take care of me."

Chapter 9

Road Trip - Mia

Mia's 2020 Toyota Camry should be the safest sedan on the road. It should be reliable. Something in her life should be reliable.

Her car is the Nightshade edition, a special, extra-sleek version of the car with black rims. Mia is staring at one of those black rims now, tracing the pattern with her eyes. The gravel digs into her knees painfully, and vaguely, she registers the smoke rising up out of her engine, billowing into the fading sky.

She can feel that she's crying, but it doesn't matter. Sobs shake her body, which makes it harder to focus, and she has the feeling that she desperately, urgently needs to keep her eyes on the black rim of her Camry.

Less than forty minutes ago, she'd walked into the living room, a duffel bag at her side, feeling jumpy. Alex had looked up from his spot on the couch, eyes widening at the sight of her.

"Babe," he'd said, cautiously, and the care he took with his tone made her furious. "What's going on?"

For a moment, she'd considered dropping the bag and crawling onto the couch with him. He was wearing a soft pair of sweatpants and an old Reid Walruses shirt. He even had a throw pillow in his lap, like he was waiting for her to join him.

"I'm going on a trip," she said, a little too loud, too brash, but she felt she couldn't waste energy on controlling her volume. Mia knew she had to fight the instinct inside her that pulled her toward inaction. Not doing anything about her problems was how she had gotten into this mess in the first place.

"...going on a trip?" Alex asked, slowly rising to his feet. He was wearing the socks she'd gotten him with tiny bananas on them. "Honey, I know you're feeling pretty bad about losing your job, but I'm not sure getting behind the wheel right now is a good idea for you. Maybe it would be better to wait for a time when you feel well. Or—maybe I could take some time off work, take you out to the cabin."

"I'm not sick, Alex," Mia said, grip tightening on the duffel bag. "I just need to gain some perspective."

"Where are you even going to go, babe?" Alex asked, taking another step toward her.

"It... I don't know. I'll just let the road take me somewhere."

"Mia, just—"

"I'm going on the fucking trip," she'd snapped, immediately feeling bad, but also feeling like she had no choice but to get out of the apartment. Something in her body was begging her to leave, and she followed that urge.

She and Sara weren't on good terms—in fact, Mia was still mad at her—but Sara would never turn her away if she showed up and asked to stay. Sara might not have been her favorite person, but a few days away from everything would do Mia good. She could feel it.

"Okay," Alex said, his voice a little more than a whisper. Mia had forgotten he was there, and blinked to bring him back into focus. It was hard to grab on to a single emotion when guilt, fear, and confusion were blending so neatly inside her.

"I'll be back in a few days," she said, ignoring the voice inside telling her to stay. Then, when she heard Alex move toward her again, she added over her shoulder, "you don't need to walk me to the car."

It started to storm five minutes into her drive, the wind whipping across the highway, sending sheets of rain slamming into her car. She'd gripped the wheel, trying to keep control, but it was so hard to see anything. She couldn't see a foot in front of her car, and found her mind drifting as she fixated on how the rain shone in the headlights.

Now, lying in the gravel, she faintly hears someone calling her name. His shouts are panicked, drifting through the wind and rain towards her and away from her.

"Mia!" Alex says, falling to his knees next to her. "Oh, Mia, I knew I shouldn't have let you go. Shit, are you hurt? Are you okay? I'm going to call an ambulance."

"No," Mia says, weakly reaching for his hand as he digs his phone from his pocket. "Can't afford an ambulance."

Alex turns his head back toward her, and now rain is dripping from the hair that's flopped over on his forehead. Mia watches it rhythmically drop onto his jacket.

A moment later, he's hoisting her into his arms and depositing her in the passenger seat of his truck. He must notice she's freezing, because he reaches over and cranks her heat, turning the vents so they're pointed right at her.

They sit quietly in his truck for a moment, and when Mia looks up, she can still see the smoke from her hood, billowing into the night, interrupted by the shards of rain pelting the ground.

"What happened?" she asks, trying to understand. She didn't remember hitting something, but she also didn't remember pulling over on the side of the road, or falling to her knees in the gravel, either. It was like her memory was a distant radio channel, fading in and out as she tried to pin it down, but it never came through clear.

"You must have lost control," Alex says, putting his hand on her thigh. "Mia, you're shaking. Here," he says, turning and reaching into the backseat. When he reappears, he's offering her a hoodie.

She's not sure if she ever stopped crying, but she feels the tears slipping down her cheeks as she pulls on his jacket. It smells devastatingly like him, like that familiar cologne, and she breathes deeply, waiting to feel better.

***

Alex's apartment building is old but stately, and Mia can pick it along the horizon as they re-enter the town. Alex maneuvers his truck into his assigned spot and turns it off, coming around the side to collect Mia, who allows him to carry her inside and up the steps to his apartment door.

He doesn't have to unlock it—he must have left in a hurry—so he can walk right in with her. He takes her to the bathroom, pulls off her wet clothes, and steps into the shower with her. Alex washes her hair, runs the warm water over her arms, rubbing at her goosebumps.

When the water starts to go cold, he turns it off and steps out, fetching a fluffy white towel from the cabinet. He wraps her in it, like her mom used to do when she was a kid, and, wrapped in his own towel, gently guides her to the bedroom.

After dressing her in one of the nice pajama sets he bought her, Alex throws on a pair of sweats and tucks her under the covers. He had the foresight to warm a heated blanket, so the spot is nice and warm as she settles in.

Mia stares at the ceiling, tracing the swirling pattern with her eyes. She tries to remember the last time she had something to eat—breakfast? Before she was fired. All she's had since is the coffee at Blanche's. That must be why she's feeling so terrible. She knows better than to have caffeine so late in the day.

"Come here," Alex says as he slips into the bed with her. He lifts his arm up and Mia snuggles into his chest, nestling her head over his heart. Despite everything that's happened tonight, it's still thrumming along at a steady beat. Mia holds her breath for a moment, and can feel her heart skipping like a rabbit's.

"Take a deep breath," Alex murmurs, his large hand running slowly up and down her back. "Try and calm down a bit. We'll regroup in the morning."

"I'm sorry," she says, and her voice breaks in the middle of "sorry."

"Shh," Alex says, "don't worry about that, love. Just try and get some sleep."

Chapter 10

Safe at Home - Mia

Mia has always loved the library. She wanders through the stacks, running her hands along the spines, listening to the sound of her breathing echoing softly against the rows and rows of books. The library is within walking distance, and Alex thought it might be good for her to get some exercise.

She peruses the cooking books, determined to find something interesting to make for Alex tonight. He likes to try new things, like her. She pulls out a few books, particularly interested in one about making homemade sourdough. She imagines Alex would enjoy homemade bread.

"Oh, Mia!"

Mia startles when the librarian catches her at the self-checkout. It's an older woman with a kind smile, but Mia can't place her. The librarian must catch her confused look, because she leads her over to the primary library desk, taking her card and books and scanning each one.

"Mia, dear, it's so good to see you. Your mother and I go way back. I miss seeing her around here, she's been bringing you in since you were so little, just to my knee," the woman says, and Mia's distracted by how her pearls clack together on her neck. Scan. Clack. Scan. Clack.

"Mia?"

She snaps her gaze away from the pearls and re-focuses on the librarian's face. Her tired eyes are kind, and it feels like they go right through her. After a second of staring, she realizes the librarian is holding the books, waiting for Mia to take them.

"Honey, you're not looking too well."

"Oh," Mia says, waving her hand, "I've been under the weather."

"I'm sorry to hear that," the librarian says, "well, I hope you can go home and get some rest."

"Not tonight," Mia says, smiling, "I have to make Alex homemade sourdough."

The librarian wrinkles her brow as Mia raises the book slightly, to provide context.

***

Somehow, Mia managed to trip on her way home, skinning her knee and bloodying the white skirt Alex bought for her.

"Baby," Alex says, later when he finds her crying because she can't get the sourdough to rise, her unbandaged knee still bleeding down her leg. "Maybe you should give the library a break."

"But—what about my books? I need to return them."

"Don't worry about that, I'll take care of it, baby. Whatever books you want I'll bring home for you."

Dread wells up inside her, but she knows Alex is right. She'll miss going to the library, but he's all she has. She clearly can't trust her own judgement right now.

Though she doesn't have health insurance, Blanche helped her schedule an appointment at a free clinic that comes to town once a month, and said she would drive her there, since her Camry was totaled after the storm. She's been staring at the calendar and marking the days until she can sit in front of a doctor and find out what's wrong with her.

In the mornings, Mia wakes up early to make coffee for Alex, who insists that she doesn't have to, but since she doesn't have a job, she wants to feel useful. She makes breakfast, which is usually just toast, then kisses him goodbye when he leaves for the mechanic shop.

Her days stretch long, so she tries to stay busy. In the first week, she'd tackled all the major projects around the apartment. The fridge (and the area behind it) were sparkling clean. The windowsills were free from dead bugs and silt. The baseboards shone and there wasn't a single cobweb left in any room.

The cookbooks were another attempt to fill her time, but anything outside of methodical cleaning feels like too much. Mia does the laundry, hating herself for how she gets excited when the dryer buzzes, alerting her to another load of laundry she can sit and fold, which will take up at least ten minutes of her time. She irons Alex's work clothes, hangs them neatly in the closet.

Now, Mia is on her hands and knees, scrubbing the area behind the toilet, trying to get a particularly sticky spot up from the floor, when something hits her shoulder and she jumps back, landing against the side of the tub.

"Oh, dear, I'm so sorry," Blanche says, putting her hand to her heart. "Scaring you scared me! I didn't mean to spook you."

Sitting on the bathroom floor, looking up at Blanche, Mia realizes this is the first time she's seen anyone but Alex in more than a week.

"Oh, don't worry about it, Blanche," Mia says, ignoring the typical bout of dizziness that sets on when she stands up. She pulls her gloves off and lays them carefully over the sink, trying to disguise the fact that she has to lean against the cabinet to stay upright. "It's so good to have company."

Mia leads Blanche out to the dining room, asking her to sit while she fetches her a cup of coffee. A moment later, Mia settles into the chair, sipping her Iced Donut coffee while Blanche takes a careful sip of hers.

"It's looking so good in here, Mia," Blanche says, "I'm half-tempted to ask you to come clean mine."

"Oh, you don't even have to ask," Mia says, putting her hand to her throat and letting out a nervous little laugh. It sounds troubled, even to her own ears. "I'm so bored, I'll clean your apartment just to get out of my head."

"Why don't you try watching TV? Or reading?"

"My brain just...can't hold on to anything. Every time I try watching TV, I fall asleep. Same with reading, except that also gives me a headache."

"That sounds terrible."

Thirty minutes later, Mia is stepping into Blanche's apartment with her rubber gloves on. She starts in the bathroom, but it's not as satisfying as cleaning Alex's because it's much cleaner. Still, she likes dusting along the top of the vanity, which Blanche clearly can't reach.

Actually, Mia can't picture Blanche cleaning, and wonders for a moment if she pays someone to come and clean her apartment for her. The building is nice enough, with a classic exterior and modern interior, and Blanche's closet is full of designer clothes—soft, buttery leather purses and form-fitting dresses. Mia thinks of the few nice blouses she owned for work, and how they didn't come anywhere close to Blanche's most worn piece.

She finds herself thinking again about Alex's childhood and all the pieces she can't fill in. He doesn't like to talk about it much because of his dad leaving, but it feels odd to her that she can't name his favorite childhood snack or list off his cherished memories. As she moves methodically room through room, she stops to look at the photos on the wall of Alex when he was a kid.

Blanche's vacuum cleaner is old and smells like burnt rubber when Mia turns it on, but she persists, vacuuming the hallway and living room rug.

"Mia, darling," Blanche says, an hour later when Mia is scrubbing at a grease stain behind the oven. "Alex is here."

Immediately embarrassed of how she looks, Mia straightens and tries to brush the hair out of her eyes. She pulls off her gloves and smooths down her shirt. Alex looks as handsome as ever in his mechanic's jumper, and Mia gives him a quick peck on the cheek.

"It looks great in here, Mom," Alex says, and Mia beams, waiting for Blanche to give her credit for the cleaning.

"Thanks, darling," Blanche says, then gestures to the two of them. "I was going to heat up some soup from a batch I made the other night, why don't you two stay for dinner? Then Mia won't have to deal with the hassle of cooking something tonight."

Mia bites her lip and wonders why Blanche didn't thank her for the cleaning, or mention her help when Alex complimented her apartment. Maybe Blanche is embarrassed that she's asked Mia to help with the cleaning, and doesn't want Alex to know. Mia feels the sudden urge to leave, and wishes she knew how to say no to Blanche's invitation.

Before she can say anything to Alex, he's sitting down on Blanche's couch and clicking on the TV, so Mia busies herself helping Blanche in the kitchen. Soon the three of them are seated around Blanche's dining room table, a chandelier that Mia just dusted twinkling above them.

Blanche holds up her wine glass. The preference for white wine must run in the family, because tonight Blanche poured a Fume Blanc that Mia finds particularly bitter. Blanche nods to Mia and Alex to clink their glasses together in a toast.

"Here's to new families," Blanche says, smiling warmly at Mia, and she softens toward the older woman. Here she is, eating with this woman who's been so kind to her, an Mia had been rude enough that she wanted to leave.

"To a new family," Mia says, smiling at them brightly and taking a long drink of her wine.

Looking at the Future - Alex

Mia tips her head back, letting her eyes flutter shut as she drinks her wine. Blanche meets Alex's gaze over the table, giving him a familiar, stern face. As always, he's the first to look away from his mother when Mia sets her wine glass on the table with an empty thunk.

"This soup is amazing," Mia says, slurring her words slightly. She grabs a roll from the basket, rips it in half, and dunks it into the bowl, sloshing a little over the side.

Alex looks down into his bowl. It's the same wedding soup his mom made at least once a week when he was growing up and always when they had guests. It's one of the few meals she knows how to make from scratch, and he's long grown tired of eating it.

But, being the dutiful son that he is, he grabs a roll and dunks it in, watching finely chopped vegetables slide off the sides and plop back into the bowl. Mia and Blanche are chatting happily about the soup and how to make it, and Alex tries to think of a way to derail the conversation so Blanche doesn't share the recipe and condemn him to the soup at home, too.

"How are you feeling, Mia?" he asks, looking up at her over his lashes, his head dipped to take a sip from his spoon.

"I'm feeling better, lately," she says, and Alex almost laughs, because, of course, she has. He's been cutting back on her dosages. He needs to hang on to most of the drug until he needs to really send her spinning, so he's been slipping just enough to keep her fuzzy. He was lucky he had the foresight to double-dose her before she tried to take her little trip, otherwise, she actually might have gotten away. Then, she says something that surprises him, "I think it might be because I stopped taking that birth control, like you said, Blanche."

The table goes quiet for a moment, and Alex looks at Mia. How had he not known that she'd stopped taking it? He knew everything else about her, and yet, he'd missed this. As they finish their meal, he keeps an eye on her.

When the meal is done and they're walking back up to his apartment, Alex slips his arm over Mia's shoulders and pulls her tightly to him. She nuzzles in right away, and Alex gets a whiff of her shampoo. He'd purchased her a new kind to smell like lilacs—which he preferred over her old rose-scented shampoo. It was a much-needed improvement.

"I've been thinking," he says once they step inside his apartment. Mia is trying to toe off her shoes, but is struggling because of the alcohol. Alex wants to laugh at the image—she doesn't realize she's been mixing pills and wine all night, which is why it's hitting her so hard.

"Yeah?" she asks, a piece of hair falling into her eyes when she looks up at him. He notices sweat on her upper lip and forehead and decides he'll need to search for the effects of Gabapentin and alcohol to make sure she'll make it through the night. The last thing he needs is for her to end up in the hospital, where they would surely test her blood and identify the substance affecting her mental state.

"Yeah," he says back, tilting his head to the side and giving her a dopey, genuine smile. He needs to make sure she's off her guard, feeling connected to him. He channels his loving boyfriend persona as he grips her elbow, giving her leverage to yank off her other shoe. "I've been thinking that maybe what you need is something to ground you. Something to give you some purpose in your days."

"I've been thinking that, too," she says, "your mom helped me set up an appointment—"

"No, not like that, Mia. I think... I think we should have a baby."

She stares at him for a moment, and he thinks he may have pushed too hard. He's usually much better at easing into what he wants, letting her think it was her idea in the first place. Now, her mouth is slightly open, her cheeks flushing pink, and he's not quite sure what she's thinking. Alex fights the urge to start talking again, knowing it's better to gauge what she's thinking first.

"A... baby?"

"Yeah," he says, grinning and her and rocking his arms like there's a bundle in them. "You know, a little person, about this big?"

"I know what a baby is, Alex," she laughs, stumbling forward into him. He catches her, wrapping his arms around her and kissing the top of her head.

"Well, what do you say about having one with me? We'd get married first, of course. You and my mother could go to pick out a dress."

When he pulls away to look at her, he notices her brow wrinkle.

"What?" he asks, placing a series of kisses along her hairline.

"Nothing," she mumbles, burying her head in his chest so her words are mumbled. "I just thought... well I always thought that when I was gonna get married, it would be a magical proposal. And growing up, I dreamed of wearing my mother's wedding dress."

Alex bites down on the inside of his cheek to contain the wave of anger that washes over him. Mia squirms in his grasp, and he realizes he's started squeezing her tighter. He forces himself to relax.

What a selfish, entitled bitch. He's taken her in, freed her of all responsibilities, and she's complaining that he didn't get down on one knee and ask for her hand in marriage? Alex is the only reason she isn't on the street, begging for change. He takes a deep breath, settling himself, before he murmurs into her hair.

"Who needs a magical proposal when we're going to have a magical marriage? We don't need all that flashy, fake stuff. We have the real thing."

Mia relaxes in his arms, apparently buying this sentiment.

"We do," she agrees, nodding her head against his sweater.

He stands like that, holding her for a minute, thinking about how easy it would be for him to break her if she tried to run from him.

"Come on," he says, then, as though he's forgotten something, "oh, shoot, actually, there's some paperwork for the apartment I was hoping you could sign quickly."

"Can I do it in the morning?" Mia says, already at the door to the bedroom. "I'm so tired I can't even think straight, let alone read."

"You don't need to read it, I already checked the whole thing. I just need your signature to show you're living here."

Mia wanders back over to him, accepting the pen he's offered her. She leans over the table and looks at the thick stack of papers he's lined up nicely. Almost absently, she runs her thumb along the stack, feathering the papers out as she does.

"This is a lot of papers for an apartment," she says, after a long moment of staring into space. Alex rolls his lips into his mouth, stifling the frustration, and nods.

"Yeah, something to do with signing a new tenant."

"I'd just feel better if I had a chance to read it. Landlords are always trying to screw people over. Actually, 44% of—"

Alex grabs her hand in a moment of fury, jamming it down so the pen leaves a hard black dot next to the signature line. She flinches back from him, and he desperately tries to pull himself back. Softening his grip on her hand, he clenches his jaw and speaks through tight lips.

"I'm tired, too, Mia, and I have to drop this off first thing in the morning. So if you could just sign it, we can both go to bed."

"Right," she says, shaking her head, her face crimson. "I'm sorry," she continues, scrawling her name on the lines as he flips through, pointing to the different areas she should sign. When it's done, he puts the cap back on the pen and places his hand on the small of her back.

"Let's go to the courthouse tomorrow," he says, "and sign the marriage license. Before I head into work. I can't wait one more second to make you my wife."

Mia looks unsure, so he swoops in, pressing his lips to hers, guiding her backwards into the bedroom before she can get in the way of his plan.

Chapter 12

Eavesdropping - Mia

Mia's humming as she chops lemons into four large quarters, nestling them around a whole chicken she's brushed with olive oil, then seasoned with salt and pepper. As an alternative to the cook books she'd wanted from the library, Alex suggested watching cooking shows instead, and now she's attempting to recreate a meal she watched and older woman put together with ease.

"Roasted chicken is the easiest thing you can make if you know how to do it right."

After adding onion and potato, Mia slides the chicken into the oven and washes her hands twice to make sure she's salmonella- free. Mia thinks of the statistics she searched when Alex brought the chicken home for her: 1.35 million cases of salmonella each year, resulting in more than 25,000 hospitalizations and 420 deaths. She would not be some fool dying because she didn't handle food properly.

Once the kitchen was back to being spotless, Mia took off her gloves and retrieved her engagement ring from the windowsill.

It was once Blanche's when she was married to Alex's dad.

"It came from my mother," Blanche had said, sliding the ring onto Mia's hand when they came back from the courthouse. "I want you to have it. I know you'll make a better marriage than my ex-husband and I could."

Now, Mia tilts her hand back and forth so the ring catches in the light. With each new sparkle she sees, her heart speeds up until it's pounding painfully against her ribcage.

It's hard to wrap her head around the fact that she's engaged to a man she met a few months ago. Unlike how she'd always dreamed of, she won't have a wedding, a bachelorette party with Sara, or her dad to walk her down the aisle. Alex says going to the courthouse will be the simplest way. They don't need a big, fancy wedding because they have each other. Mia agrees with him out loud, but deep down, she knows she's vain because she wants everyone to see her walk down the aisle. Growing up, she'd always dreamed of picking out her dress with her mom, hosting a rehearsal dinner, and fighting playfully with her partner over what the color scheme should be. She even dreamed about dealing with a monster of a mother-in-law, who would try to take over the planning, and a fiancé who would tell her to back off.

Now, Mia thinks about signing her name at the courthouse, which reminds her of the apartment documents she'd almost ruined the other night.

"What's that?" she'd asked, pointing to the large black splotch on the top page.

Alex had picked the stack up, tucking it into a folder and then into his work bag. From the look on his face, Mia could tell that she had done something stupid. She just couldn't remember what it was.

"Don't worry about it, love. You were just a little tipsy last night."

Mia flushed again, thinking about it. She never used to get drunk—statistically, alcohol consumption led to higher rates of cancer, so she only had the occasional glass of wine. She couldn't even remember how much she'd had to drink at Blanche's the other night, but it was clear she needed to cut back. She couldn't control herself around alcohol anymore.

Despite the incident with the wine, she had been feeling more like herself, like she told Alex. She thinks about his suggestion that they have a baby, and that they have already started trying, and puts a hand to her stomach. Suddenly, bile rises up her throat and she dashes to the bathroom, heaving over the bleach-smelling bowl.

After rinsing her mouth and scrubbing the toilet again, she washes her hands once more, then puts them to her head. She couldn't be pregnant already, right?

As she thinks about being pregnant, she starts to feel light-headed, and wishes she could call her mom. She would know what to do, would know if this nausea was random or related to a baby.

Wanting the next best thing, Mia takes a deep breath, pulls on a hoodie, and steps out into the hallway to talk to Blanche. Alex asked Mia to always text him when she was heading to his mother's apartment, but Mia decides not to this time. She isn't sure if he's told Blanche, or if he wants to wait, but Mia needs reassurance from another woman right now.

She needs a mother to tell her she's ready to take care of a baby. Plus, she'll just make sure she's back home before Alex gets back from the shop, and he won't know the difference. Mia can ask Blanche to keep it their secret until Alex is ready to tell her.

The apartment hallway smells like everyone's dinner mixed together, with just a hint of dog pee that's soaked into the carpets. Mia wonders if she should try and scrub the carpet in their hallway, to get rid of the odor. Alex would probably like it smelling nice when he was walking in after work.

As Mia nears Blanche's doorway, she hears multiple voices inside and pauses, not wanting to disturb Blanche if she has friends over. Then again, it would be nice to see someone other than Alex and Blanche, Mia thinks, and inches closer to the door.

She's still trying to decide if she should knock or not when she catches her own name—"Mia"—said in a low, malicious tone. The anxiety boiling low in her stomach rockets right up to her throat, and she places a hand on her neck, trying to soothe the feeling.

It's Alex's voice on the other side of the door, and he sounds angry. She decides to stay and listen—if she can figure out what she's done, why he's so upset, she might be able to solve the problem before he gets to their apartment.

Moving slowly, avoiding the creaky floorboard to the right of Blanche's door, Mia moves close to the heavy wood, trying to make out specific words.

"I got suspended on that stupid app, and I haven't been able to log back into my other account."

"You don't have to keep that up. It did the trick."

"Yes, but I quite enjoy letting out some of my frustration online. I can see why people like to do it."

"Are you sure she hasn't figured out it's you?"

"Of course not, I'm a doll to her face every day. Wish she would give me a break from the constant visits."

Mia shifts forward a bit more, heart pounding. What are they talking about? Mia didn't even know Blanche knew how to use the internet. And who was she leaving hate comments for?

"Well, it shouldn't be much longer now. I'm going to try and get into the courthouse this week. I have to get her on a day she's lucid enough that it won't tip people off."

Suddenly, everything feels too loud. Mia can hear her heart like it's pressed right up against her eardrums. Her hands go numb, and she has to squeeze them to nudge some feeling back to her fingers. They are talking about her. Blanche and Alex are talking about Mia—about leaving her hate comments. About taking her to the courthouse.

The floor beneath Mia's feet begins to tilt and she wills her body to stay upright. She needs to hear the rest of what they're going to say. Surely there's a reason they would be talking like this. Mia thinks of Blanche, so sweet, hugging her and telling her everything would be okay. Blanche wasn't capable of leaving nasty hate comments on her posts.

You're a disgusting skank.

Fat ugly slut.

You should kill yourself, whore.

"Wonderful. I don't know how much longer I can stand listening to her complain all the time."

"Lucky for her parents they don't have to listen to her anymore."

"Oh, you never told me about what happened with him."

"It was nothing. When he came by, I just told him she didn't live here. Said she left that night, didn't know what had happened to her."

Mia startled. Her dad had come to the apartment? And Alex said she wasn't home—lied about her living here at all. Was her dad looking for her?

"What happened to her car?"

"Taken for parts. It's likely in a million pieces by now."

"Good riddance. That thing was hideous. I don't know why you would let your daughter drive such an ugly car if you have the money to give her something of quality. Clearly, her parents don't know what to do with all that money. At least once we have it, I won't be caught dead driving a Toyota."

Blanche said "Toyota" the same way someone else might say "car crash." Mia might have laughed if she wasn't so panicked. Suddenly she wished Sara was here with her now, hearing this too. So Mia could know for sure this was real, that she wasn't imagining this conversation. Was that possible? Could she hallucinate an entire conversation?

"Well, if that daughter is Mia—"

"Did you hear something?" Blanche's voice is high and sharp, and Mia has to move away from the door quickly. Had she shifted? Hit the squeaky plank?

Blanche's heels click as she nears the door, and Mia looks up and down the hallway. There's a stairwell on either side of the building. If one of them comes after her and she makes the wrong choice, they'll catch her running up the stairs. They'll know she was listening.

There's no time to think. Mia chooses a direction at random and slips off her shoes, sprinting down the hall as fast as she can. She gently closes the door to the stairwell just as Blanche's apartment door creaks open. Going on her toes, she takes the stairs two at a time, chest heaving when she finally gets to the top. She throws the door open and races to the apartment.

Her hands shake as she tries to fit her key into the lock. If he's moving quickly, Alex could be opening the door to the hall any second. She tries not to picture the look on his face if he saw her out here, holding her shoes. Clearly hiding something.

She nearly cries out with relief when the door swings open and she dashes in, closing it quietly behind her and hanging her key on the hook, where it always lives. Nothing can be out of place, or Alex will know.

For a moment, she leans against the door, hand to her mouth, trying to catch her breath. Tears track, unbidden, down her cheeks. She feels like she might suffocate. She feels like her body is an earthquake she can't get control over.

Then she hears Alex's key in the lock.

If he gets a good look at her, standing here like this, crying, he'll know she was listening—and then what? She thinks backwards to his tight hugs, the way he's gripped her arms, how he grabs the back of her head when he kisses her.

She thinks about her car, her statistically safe sedan, separated into a million pieces. No way to escape. Like she never existed at all. Mia realizes at once that Alex had no reason to come after her that night, and yet she never questioned when he showed up like her knight in shining armor. She didn't call for help. Alex had been following her.

Mia sets her shoes down in their usual spot and runs on her toes to the bathroom, heart pounding in her throat. Once inside, she cranks the water faucet in the shower to hot and closes the door as quietly as she can. Still trying to control her breathing, she strips off her clothes, shoving them haphazardly into the laundry hamper.

"Mia?" Alex calls, dangerously close to the bathroom. She leaps into the shower, cursing under her breath at the scalding hot water as it sears her skin, but she keeps the water at the highest temp, hoping it might steam the room faster and give the illusion that she's been showering for a long time. the water as hot as it would go, hoping it would steam faster and create the illusion that she had been in the bathroom for a long time. Wincing at the temperature, she ducked her head under the water, and quickly lathered shampoo.

"Mia," Alex said again, opening the door to the bathroom. Mia hummed under her breath, squirting soap onto her loofah and rubbing it down her arms, over her stomach. Alex cracked the shower curtain, peeking in at her.

He often came to check on her in the shower, and she would smile at him, giggle as he reached in for her. She has to smile at him now. She has to seem normal.

"Hey, baby," she says, flicking some of the shampoo on her fingers in his direction. He doesn't smile at her. Her heart skips in her chest.

"What are you doing?" he asks, eyes tracing up and down her face. "Why are you in the shower? Don't you have something in the oven?"

Mia gives him a blank stare, then looks down at the shampoo on her fingers. She can use her lack of clarity lately to her advantage.

"I don't... I don't think so. Did you see something in there?"

"There's a whole fucking chicken in the oven, Mia." Alex's voice is hard as he stares at her, and she can't help it—she bursts into tears. Her sobs come so fast and hard that it takes her a moment to notice that Alex has turned the water off and is wrapping a towel around her shoulders.

"I'm sorry baby, shh," he's saying, bundling her up and taking her into his arms. Her arms twitch, urging her to push him away. Thinking of the cold, dead tone he'd used when talking to his mother. How he'd said her name like he hated her.

"I think I'm pregnant, Alex," is what she says instead, the words shocking even her. He pulls back from her, his eyes flitting back and forth between hers.

"You're pregnant?"

Mia hates the wide look in his eyes, genuine astonishment. He's playing the happy boyfriend so well, beaming at her like this is the best thing that's ever happened to him.

"I mean, I don't know for sure, but I'm just feeling so emotional, and I threw up this morning. I think... I'd like to sign the marriage papers at the courthouse as soon as possible. It feels weird to be pregnant and not married."

"I agree, baby," Alex says, kissing the top of her head. She realizes that this is something he does a lot, and it's because he usually curls her body into him so his arms are completely around her. When he has her wrapped up like this, she couldn't escape if she wanted to.

Before she can lose her resolve and shove away, the smell of smoke trickles into the bathroom, and Alex swears under his breath right before the smoke alarm starts to blare.

Chapter 13

Time to Find the Me That's Gone - Mia

It's five in the morning, and Mia's heart is racing so fast she's afraid Alex is going to wake up and realize something's wrong. Each time he looked at her last night, she felt like he was looking right through her, like I know what you're doing was emblazoned on her forehead.

Mia is on her back, her hands laced together on her stomach, staring up at the ceiling. For a long time after getting in bed with Alex last night, she'd thought about what she heard, playing it over and over in her head, trying to determine if there was a way it could be innocent, a way that she could have misinterpreted the whole thing.

I don't know how much longer I can stand listening to her complain all the time.

Now, with the morning light just starting to peek through the blinds, Mia knows the truth—Alex and his mother are bad people.

If she's honest with herself, the worst part isn't even Alex himself—though that obviously stings—it's the fact that she was so honest and open with Blanche, sharing things with her that Mia had never even told her own mother. The betrayal sat like hot oil in her stomach, increasing her nausea and fueling her anger.

To pass the time, Mia catalogs everything she's lost because of Alex and his mother: her relationship with her parents, her best friend, her beautiful house, her job, and her credibility in the town where she grew up. People here will think of her differently forever because of their actions.

She thinks of the iPhone that mysteriously landed in her purse, and knows without a doubt in her mind that it was Alex setting her up.

Her hands itch, wanting to hit Alex, push him off the bed so she can scramble out of there, but she knows she has to be careful. This isn't a man who lost his temper and punched a wall—this is a man who carefully planned to take her independence from her.

After throwing up the morning before, she's felt her head get clearer and clearer, and with nothing but a burnt chicken for dinner, she decided just to skip eating altogether, claiming nausea. Though her stomach is sickeningly hollow, her brain feels better than it had in months.

She knows what she has to do—she has to wait for Alex to leave, then get out of the apartment as quickly as she can. Without a vehicle, she'll have to make a visit to her parent's storage unit with her fingers crossed that her dad's ancient Chevy Camaro will still run.

Her mind races making plans, ironing out details. Alex is smart, clearly, as he's already gotten her into this situation. But Mia knows she's smarter. All she has to do is not let him realize she's onto him.

Remembering back to that first time they met, on the side of the road, it's like she can hear him saying "Yeah, name's Dave. He's a part-time fry cook, part-time private detective."

How much truth is there to that? If she does leave, will Alex get a private detective on her tail right away?

As though he senses her thinking about him, Alex rolls over, throwing an arm over her and pulling her close. She ignores the instinct to stiffen up, and instead snuggles into him like she normally would, ignoring the way her stomach flips at the contact.

Does she even know him at all?

"G'morning, love," he murmurs into her hair, tugging her hips even closer to his.

"Good morning," she says, hoping her voice doesn't betray her. Alex's hands roam over her body, and she has to take deep breaths to keep from flinching. When his fingers start to skirt under the hem of her shirt, she feels bile rise in her throat and bolts up from the bed, running to the bathroom. With the door closed, she vomits into the bowl, but almost nothing comes up. There's nothing left in her stomach.

Mia flushes the toilet, her hand on her stomach, roiling at the thought that she could be pregnant with his baby. But is the nausea from pregnancy, stress, or something else? Mia wishes she could call Sara to ask about morning sickness, and presses her hand to her forehead, mourning the loss of her best friend.

When she shuffles back into the room, Alex is propped up on his elbows, watching her. She stares at her side of the bed, knowing she needs to climb back in next to him, like she's been doing every morning.

"Sorry," she says, sliding back under the covers.

"That's okay, baby," he says, rolling over and putting his arm under her head. Her heart is pounding, adrenaline pulsing through her veins. It's like the feeling right before a roller coaster takes off, and you're sitting there wondering if you've just signed your death wish. Being in bed with Alex feels like entering the fighting ring with a bear, or dunking into the ocean in a shark cage.

"I've just been feeling kind of nauseous lately," she says, rubbing her hand over her stomach and moving slightly away from him.

"I'm sorry, love," he says, running his hand over her hair and feeling her forehead for a moment. "You do feel a bit warm. Maybe I should stay home with you today."

Mia forces herself to stay perfectly still, to not betray how badly she wants him to leave the apartment. If he stays home for the day, that will be another twenty-four hours spent in his presence, forcing herself to act like she still likes him. Even sick, he might want to be intimate with her, and she can't stand the thought. She needs him to leave, or she'll slip up and betray her true feelings.

"I think… I think I should take a pregnancy test," she says, "to really know whether the nausea is from that or something else."

"Oh," Alex says, miming smacking his hand against his forehead. "I hadn't even thought of that. You know what? I'll run to the drugstore right now and get you one. Do you want anything else?"

"Crackers," she says, clutching the blanket in both hands. He's only running to the drug store. She has maybe twenty minutes—max—before he's walking right back through the front door. "And, also—well, never mind."

"What is it, love?" he asks, turning in the middle of pulling on a fresh shirt. His face is so considerate and open that she almost forgets what she heard the night before. "If you want something, I'll get it for you."

"It's silly."

"Nothing is silly if it's for you. What is it?" his voice is starting to get the hard edge to it that creeps in when he's annoyed with her. Mia waits for her anxiety about his mood to rise up, but she realizes she doesn't care if he's upset anymore.

"Well, you know that tea place in the mall? They have a really good nausea blend with peppermint that my mom used to get for me."

"In the mall? That's on the other side of town."

"You're right, it was a stupid idea."

Alex stares at her as he collects his wallet and keys from the table. They stay like that for a moment, Alex poised to go and Mia half-sitting up in bed, swallowing against the persistent nausea that has her mouth watering and her sides cramping.

"Okay," he says, finally, leaning forward to give her a kiss on the top of the head. "I'll be back."

Of course, he didn't commit to going to the tea shop, so Mia doesn't know how long he'll be gone. She listens to the thud of his feet as he moves through the kitchen, and then him putting his boots on, then the door latching, and the key in the lock.

For a moment, she stays in bed, convinced he'll turn around the second she moves, having forgotten something. After a minute, she slowly creeps to the window, moving the curtain as minimally as she can, peering through the smallest sliver.

Alex's truck is pulling out of the parking spot.

She lets the curtain fall back into place and turns around, staring at the room for a moment, her body vibrating with nervous energy.

Mia has two options: she can wait, get through the day, and prepare to leave tomorrow when Alex goes back to work, or she can get out right now. Going tomorrow would give her the whole day's head start on him, but going now means she doesn't have to pretend to be in love with him.

The clock above the bed ticks loudly, and Mia jolts into action.

First, she grabs her black backpack from the closet. She stares at the closet, realizing Alex has completely remade her wardrobe. Gone are the simple black and neutral clothes, and in their place are polka dots, sparkles, and bright patterns. If she wears these, she'll be spotted immediately.

Instead, she opens his drawer and takes two pairs of sweatpants and two of his tops. She packs bras, underwear, and socks alongside his clothes, throws in her travel bag and toothbrush, and zips the bag. When she glances up at the clock, she realizes ten minutes have already passed. If he's just running to the drugstore, he could already be checking out.

Cursing under her breath, Mia quickly tosses in her wallet, passport, and the little cash she has in her end table. She runs to the dining table, sliding in her laptop, chargers, and a notebook, then remembers her birth certificate in the fire safe under Alex's bed.

After a moment, she decides to leave it. She can always get another.

Mia hurries to the kitchen, dumping a box of granola bars, a bag of beef jerky, and two bottles of water into the bag. When she makes it to the door of the apartment, fifteen minutes have passed. She has five minutes until the soonest Alex could be back, but fifteen more if he's gone to the tea shop for her.

She puts on her sneakers and pushes through the apartment door.

It's not until she's at the bottom of the stairwell, about to walk out the back door of the building, that she realizes she's forgotten the key to her dad's storage unit. She glances at the time on her watch—it's been nineteen minutes since Alex left. He could be pulling back into the parking lot any second.

Mia wavers, unsure if she should take the chance to go or run back up the stairs. What can she do without her dad's car? She needs transportation to get away from Alex.

She tucks her bags under the stairwell, taking out the key to the apartment and sprinting back up the steps, taking them two at a time. As she approaches the door, she realizes Alex could already be back inside, so she stops to listen, but hears nothing.

Hands shaking, she unlocks the door and steps inside, still hearing nothing. When she's sure he isn't home, she runs to the bedroom and grabs her jewelry case from under her side of the bed. It has the key to the storage unit, and, worst case scenario, she can always pawn some of her jewelry to make some quick cash.

Once she has the storage key, she just wants to sprint back out, leaving the deadbolt unlocked, but that will immediately clue Alex in that something's wrong, so she takes an extra second to lock it back up. Mia glances over her shoulder as she runs back to the stairwell, racing down and heaving a sigh of relief when she sees her backpack and weekend bag right where she left them.

When she pushes the back door to the apartment open and steps out into the sunshine, she feels something lift off her chest. She's made it out. She's going to be okay.

Until she rounds the corner and sees Alex striding toward her, bag in tow. She immediately backpedals, putting a hand to her mouth to keep from making noise. Why is he coming in through the back door? Did he see her?

She continues backing up until she's rounded the other side of the building, and presses her back up against the brick. She needs him to go inside.

Mia wonders if she should keep going around to the front, but she's on the longer side of the building now. If Alex is still walking toward her, she won't make it around the corner before he sees her.

Her eyes dart to the line of trees pushing up against the property. She won't make it around the corner before he sees her, but she could disappear into woods.

Mia strains her ears, trying to hear if Alex is coming toward her, or if he's opening the door and going inside. She decides she's not going to wait and find out. Sliding up the wall so she's completely out of eyeshot from the back door, she sprints towards the trees. It's weeds up to her knees and uneven ground, but she doesn't stop until she can't see the building when she looks back.

Chapter 14

The Escape Plan - Mia

As Mia stumbles her way through the trees and shrubs, she tries to figure out what Alex is doing. What would she do if she were him?

She'll need to get on a road to get to her dad's storage unit. It makes sense that after Alex realized she was gone, and had taken her passport and wallet, he would get right back into his truck. Knowing him, he's probably spitting mad, driving up and down the streets around their apartment way too fast, revving the big engine on that truck.

Mia's suddenly grateful she's struggling through the woods. If she'd walked along the road, like she planned, he probably would have found her right away.

And then, suddenly, she's out of the trees and standing in a grassy clearing. Just ahead of her, about twenty feet away up a steep hill, is the highway. She realizes it's the same stretch of road where she first got that flat tire. The memory of Alex then is so different from the reality. What would be different if he hadn't happened to come across her that day on the road? Would she still have her job? Would she still be living in her house, with all the features she loved?

She swallows the lump in her throat and raises her hand to her eyes, making a quick decision. If she follows the highway, she thinks she can pick the right exit and make it to the storage unit, which is her next step. Her phone is turned off in her backpack with the location turned off, but she doesn't want to risk draining the battery in case she needs it, so she follows her intuition and heads north, staying just inside the line of trees in case Alex might be driving past on the road above.

****

Gone Mia: Deadly Deception

When Mia finally sees the familiar Smith Storage sign outside the complex, she nearly collapses in relief. It's been thirteen hours since she left the apartment, and she only stopped once to rest, eating a granola bar and some jerky from her bag. She'd expected to be nauseous again, but surprisingly, she managed to keep the food down and is trying to ignore the pangs of hunger rippling through her stomach now.

She approaches the gate at the front of the complex, holding her breath as she punches in the old password: her birthday. To her relief, it beeps once and the gate swings open.

Mia slips inside and walks along the pavement until she finds her dad's unit. With the key, she's in easily, and gropes around the inside the wall to find the light. Once it flickers on, she's looking at her dad's old Camaro under a black dust cover. To the left of the Camaro are a few antique pieces and several tubs with unknown contents.

It takes her a minute to pull the dust cover off, then she's running her hand over the pearly paint, trying to remember the last time her dad got this car out of the garage. It takes her a moment, but she finds the both the keys and the garage door opener in the glove box. She opens the door, then sticks the key in and turns it, closing her eyes.

If the car doesn't start, she doesn't know what she's going to do.

But it purrs to life, rumbling warmly under her feet. Nearly collapsing over the steering wheel in relief, she reverses out of the storage unit, parks the Camaro, returns to the unit to lock it up, and slides back into the driver's seat a moment later.

Her dad let her drive the Camaro when she turned eighteen, and it was considered a very special treat. She wonders how he would feel about her driving it now, if he would faint at the idea of her behind the wheel without him.

She feels a rogue sob lodge in her throat. Her dad would want her to be safe. Her dad came to the apartment looking for her—he was right about Alex the whole time.

Mia thinks again about her phone in her backpack and resists the urge to turn it on. She made sure to turn her location off, so hopefully if Alex is tracking her, it still shows her as being at home, but it still feels risky.

She could call her parents, but she doesn't know the extent of Alex and Blanche's plan. Mia doesn't want to put her parents in danger if she can help it.

The highway stretches out in front of her, nearly empty with the exception of a few eighteen-wheelers puttering along. Mia knows the best thing she can do is put miles between her and Alex. As she gets further from home, the total number of locations increases, making it more difficult for Alex to find her. She presses the accelerator.

A few hours later, she's too tired to keep her eyes open, and pulls off into a truck stop. She goes inside to use the bathroom and uses some of her cash to fill up the tank and buy a cold turkey sandwich. She eats the sandwich at a booth inside the stop, then quickly brushes her teeth in the bathroom.

The backseat of the Camaro isn't the comfiest place she's slept, but her body is already relaxing at the thought that Alex is far, far away.

***

A bright light wakes Mia up and she rubs her eyes, realizing the light is sunlight streaming through the back windshield. In a moment, she's sitting up, looking around dazedly, trying to get her bearings.

Mia goes back into the truck stop to brush her teeth and change into Alex's clothes. She has to pull the sweatpants as tight as they'll go, and the shirt is a little big on her, but it's not as bad as she thought it might be. After using hand soap for a sink-bath and finger-combing her hair, she goes back to the Camaro.

Trucks and cars flow in and out of the stop, and Mia keeps her head low, eyes darting around just in case she sees Alex's truck. It's not likely that he would end up at this exact truck stop—and she's sure she never told him about her dad's Camaro—but she can't ignore the possibility.

Gone Mia: Deadly Deception

Despite the paranoia in the back of her head, she can't help but feel her spirits lifted as she makes her way back to the car. The sun is shining and the air is surprisingly crisp. Birds chirp and hop around the trees to her left, and a family pulls in, laughing and talking about snacks as they head inside.

With so much space between her and Alex, she realizes the world doesn't exist in the tiny, sick circle she'd drawn around herself.

Her stomach is growling, but her head is clear. The fuzzy feeling that's been hanging around her for weeks has finally disappeared, and she's grateful for that. She wonders if it's the adrenaline finally pushing away the fog.

Mia finally powers her phone back on. She has 67 missed calls from Alex, and a slew of texts.

Baby, where are you?

Mia, are you okay?

Where did you go?

Why aren't my messages delivering to your phone?

Mia, what the fuck.

You can't just leave like that.

Are you at your parents' house?

Answer your fucking phone.

This is really how you're going to treat me?

Yeah, sure, treat me like shit. Nobody else will ever want you.

ANSWER YOUR PHONE

You need to come home, Mia.

Where are you?

I'm coming for you.

The last message sends a shudder down her back, and she glances around again, feeling sure she's about to look right into Alex's eyes on the other side of the parking lot. She's too easy to spot, too recognizable, even in Alex's clothes.

Mia double-checks to ensure her location-tracking is off, then connects it to the phone charger and steers back onto the highway. The sun is fully up over the horizon now, washing the trees and fields to either side of her in a golden glow. Commuters zip around her, on their way to work. Trucks and delivery people yawn into their hands. Mia struggles to keep her anxiety at bay as she drives alongside them.

An hour later, she's pulling off again and finding a branch of parents' bank. Her checking account may be at an all-time low, but she can access her shared savings account. It's technically for school, and she was given access when she started her associate degree, but her parents will understand her withdrawing some of the money now.

The teller eyes her up and down, clearly judging her outfit, but hands over they money when Mia knows the account password and shows her I.D. Once she's back in the car, Mia divides the cash between her wallet, backpack, and weekend bag, then stashes some in her bra, sock, and the glove box.

With cash at hand, Mia starts to relax. She might actually be able to pull this off. Taking the highway again, she drives and doesn't stop until Atlanta sparkles on the horizon.

***

Mia flinches when a store bell jingles overhead ringing throughout the shop. Her eyes connect with a woman standing at the counter, arms crossed. She looks Mia up and down, raising her eyebrows.

"Can I help you?"

Every wall in the store is lined with mannequin heads from floor to ceiling, in every color and style you can imagine. Mia struggles to focus on the attendant, rather than taking it all in.

"Yeah," Mia says, trying to infuse her voice with confidence. "I... I need to buy a wig. Or a few, actually."

"What do you need a wig for?"

Mia pulls back, shocked at the woman's tone. She's clearly distrustful, and Mia wonders for a moment if she should turn around and get back in her car. It might be easier to find wigs at a costume shop, or pop-up Halloween store.

"Are you okay?" the woman asks again, a hint of concern in her steely voice.

To her surprise, a ball forms in her throat, tears welling up in her eyes. She didn't realize how badly she wanted someone to ask her if she was okay. Mia blinks rapidly and presses her lips together, not wanting to break down in front of this stranger.

"Oh," the woman says, slowly uncrossing her arms and coming around the counter. She stands a few feet away, giving Mia another hard look. Whatever she sees, her entire demeanor softens, and her voice is low when she speaks. "I see. You're not coming in here to mess around, are you? You're trying to keep someone from seeing you."

Mia looks up at her and their gazes hold for a moment. Something passes between them, and for the first time since she met Alex on the side of the highway, Mia feels like she's not alone in her situation.

"You don't want to look like yourself," the woman continues says.

When Mia nods, ever-so-slightly, the woman turns on her heel, gesturing for Mia to follow her into the shop.

"I'm Evalyn. You don't have to tell me your name. Come on, let's get you something in here."

When Mia leaves, it's wearing a brand new copper wig with straight bangs across her forehead. She hardly recognized herself in the mirror when Evalyn turned it around for her to look.

"Have you ever worn a wig before?" she'd asked, and when Mia shook her head again, Evalyn sighed and started grabbing supplies. It took them about an hour, but with enough instruction, Mia felt confident she could pull it off.

She climbs back into the Camaro with the long copper wig on her head and a short black bob in her bag, which also has supplies for application and care. Both the wigs she now had were so different from her mousy, shoulder-length hair, which is probably why Evalyn suggested them.

"Doing your makeup different can help, too," Evalyn had said, as she showed Mia how to use the glue on her head. "Men aren't very perceptive, when it really comes down to it."

Mia had tried to give her a generous tip, sensing she was speaking from experience, but Evalyn had pushed it back toward her, shaking her head.

"You need this more than I do, sweetheart. Be safe."

Now, Mia finds a cheap motel on the outskirts of Atlanta and pays in cash. She parks the Camaro out of sight, hoping it won't be vandalized or stolen. Despite the stiff mattress and dingy room, she sleeps better than she has in months.

Chapter 15

Tracking - Alex

The second Alex walked into the apartment, he could tell something was off. It only took him a second to realize Mia's laptop was not at the table like usual, and it set him off.

Rage already climbing up his throat, he'd slammed into the bedroom, only to find the bed empty, the drawers pulled open, her bag missing from the closet.

Letting out an expletive, Alex slammed his fist against the closet door, which splintered easily under the force. He kicked an errant shoe across the room. How could he have let her go this easily?

That flash he'd seen just outside the building—was that her? Dropping the bag with the pregnancy test on the floor, he'd turned on his heel and raced down the steps, breathing heavily. He ran up and down the sidewalk in either direction in front of the house, breathing hard and angrily when he didn't see her.

His truck was still in its place. She didn't take it. So she was going on foot. But where?

"Hello?" Blanche said, picking up on the first ring. "Alex, what's wrong? Aren't you at work?"

"No," he'd said, forcing the word out between his teeth. "Mia said she thought she was pregnant this morning, so I went to get her a pregnancy test. I just got back—and she's gone. Her shit is gone."

"Alex, calm down," his mother said, sounding unbothered. "She has no reason to suspect anything. I'm sure this is just a misunderstanding. Just text her and figure out where she is. It's like when she took off in her car."

Except it wasn't like that. Alex could tell.

His texts were becoming increasingly more aggressive the longer she didn't answer him. He'd checked the location-tracking app he'd installed on her phone, but it showed she was still at the apartment.

"She's not answering," he said, calling his mother right back.

"You said she took her stuff?" Blanche said, and Alex could practically see her pinching his nose. Irritation coursed through him, centering in his chest. His mother could act like nothing was wrong now, but he could tell. Something was off. Mia had figured it out.

"Yes," Alex said, having climbed back up the stairs. He pushed back into the apartment, taking stock of everything that was gone. Her wallet. Her passport. He cursed himself for not taking them sooner.

"Well, didn't Dave give you those little things?"

With a jolt, Alex remembered the little trackers Dave had given him. And he'd put one in the lining of Mia's bag. Relief flooded through him. "Oh, my God, yes," he said, and he immediately got off the phone with his mother.

The only problem with the tracker is that he hadn't bothered to ask Dave about using it at the time. It took him hours before he could reach Dave, who had to hurry back from a job to help him. Alex fed him a lie about Mia stealing his stuff and taking off, and Dave bought it, helping him identify the tracker.

At that point, Mia had a whole day on him, giving her a chance to get out of the city.

Now, Alex stares at the little blinking dot on his phone. It's been at a motel for a few hours now, so that must be where Mia is.

At first, when he'd seen the dot moving along the highway, he'd asked Dave to check bus tickets in the area. No hits for Mia. Either she used a fake name or got her hands on a car.

But her Camry was in pieces, spread across a few different junkyards. Where in the world did she get a car? She could have stolen it, but Alex couldn't imagine her doing that. Would she even know how to hotwire a car?

Her having a car was a problem. First, because it gave her the ability to put distance between them. Secondly, she may have told someone what she knew to get the car. Her parents? Sara? Alex thought he'd done a good job of isolating her, but there was a chance her dad was still holding out hope. He had come to the apartment, after all.

Alex wants to race to the hotel, but he's conscious of not wanting to get a ticket, so he keeps the speedometer only a few miles above the legal limit. Soon, he turns into the motel parking lot, his heart picking up speed. He's so close to that little green dot. Now, all he has to do is wait for Mia to come out and grab her when she least expects it. It's still dark out as his fingers drum the steering wheel in anticipation.

Somewhere, deep down, he has to admit he's impressed with her. He certainly didn't think she had it in her to get away.

Thinking of the pregnancy test he abandoned on the floor of their bedroom, he wonders if she's actually pregnant or if the whole thing was a lie. His heart squeezes—what a horrible thing to lie about.

The sun is just coming up as he watches the motel's inhabitants. A couple rounds the corner, their arms looped around each other, giggling as they fall into a room. Half an hour later, a guy in a baggy sweatshirt wanders up to a door, knocks on it, and is passed something by the person inside.

Alex watches the activity with a scowl on his face. It's disgusting that Mia chose a place like this—she must feel like a criminal just staying in a room next to these people. Every time a door opens, Alex's eyes dart to the door, watching the person until they pass by.

The door directly in front of his truck opens, and a woman comes out. It seems like she's looking right at him, and he slants his glance to the right, not wanting anyone to go to the front office about a creepy guy in the parking lot, as unlikely as that may be when the whole place is filled with creepy people. When the woman has gotten a few steps away, he glances at her again. Wearing all black, limping slightly. Short brown hair. Nope, not Mia.

Alex returns to watching, sipping the coffee in his cup holder. Another hour passes, the sun rises, and still, there's no sight of Mia. Starting to get agitated, he pulls his phone out again. That dot is still in the same place, blinking just in front of him. Taking a deep breath, he climbs out of the truck. He's tired of waiting.

"Hey," he says, approaching the man at the front, who looks like he's half asleep. The guy blinks sleepily at him.

"Hey," he replies, "we're full."

"I'm not looking for a room," Alex says, grimacing at the idea. "I'm looking for a woman."

"Sorry, man," the guy says, shaking his head and already turning away. "Policy. I can't tell you about any of the guests. Just try calling her."

Alex doesn't want to do this, but he pulls a fake badge from his pocket, flashes it at the guy, and lowers his voice.

"If you don't tell me which room she's in," Alex says, voice low and serious. "I'll charge you with obstruction of justice and drag you into the station right now. Policy."

The guy stares at him for a moment, eyes darting between his fake badge and a duffel bag on the floor. Alex notices this.

"What's that?" Alex says, looking pointedly at the bag. "Something special in there?"

"No—" the guy says too quickly before turning and tapping something into the computer. "Name?"

"Mia Agostini."

"Sorry, man," the guy says a moment later, turning with his hands up. "Nobody here under that name."

Alex swears, slamming his badge against the counter. The man behind the counter looks frightened.

"Print it out," Alex says, gesturing at the computer. "Just give me the list. Now."

The guy swallows and looks for a moment like he might protest, but Alex gives the bag on the floor another pointed look. A moment later, the printer is whirring.

Alex snatches the paper from his hands and stalks out of the office, scanning the list. The attendant wasn't lying—Mia's name isn't on the paper. Alex checks his phone again. She's here, so where the heck is she?

He lets out a low noise and slaps the paper down on the roof of his truck, looking it over again. Then, he sees something that makes him pause.

Blanche Bartlett.

Room 103. Alex turns, letting the paper blow away in the wind, searching the room numbers on the peeling doors. No—it can't be.

Angry, he stalks forward, kicking in the door directly in front of his truck. The door he's spent the last three hours staring at. He immediately sees Mia's bag, some cash on the table, and a strange bag on the desk. He grabs it, rips it open, breaks the zipper, and pulls out the contents, letting it dangle from his hand.

A red wig with bangs.

Cursing, Alex throws the wig across the room, snatching her backpack from the floor. He starts searching through it. He checks his phone again. This is why it showed she was still here—she left everything behind. Including the tracker.

On the one hand, it's good because it means she's without her wallet, passport, and cash. How far can she get? Alex reaches into the bag's laptop sleeve and feels around until his hand lands on the tracker. He rips it out and looks at it. The tracker is useless to him.

He now has no way of knowing where she is. And he saw that woman with the brown hair walking out of this hotel room hours ago. That must have been Mia. He curses himself for being a fool.

Before the attendant can come and charge him for the door, Alex scoops up Mia's belongings and climbs back into his truck, slamming the door behind him.

Chapter 16

A Good Place to Hide - Mia

When bright and overpowering headlights shone through her blinds, Mia rolled over in bed, ripped from a restful sleep. Despite the adrenaline of the situation, she was getting better sleep every night. Being away from Alex was clearing her head.

The headlights went away soon enough, but Mia couldn't fall back to sleep. She went to the bathroom and climbed back onto the bed—above the covers. As hard as she tried, her body just wouldn't let her go back to sleep.

Finally, sighing, she'd decided to go to the vending machine for trail mix, thinking of her mom.

A midnight snack is the best way to fall back asleep, she remembers her mom saying, and giggling as she pulled a pint of ice cream from the freezer. Mia sat on the counter, watching with rapt attention as her mom scooped a large helping into each bowl.

She wouldn't be able to get ice cream from the vending machine—but maybe she needed something other than beef jerky and granola bars if she wanted to fall back to sleep. She made a note to get a real breakfast the next morning.

Her hand landed on the doorknob, but something in her told her not to leave. After a moment, she turned, pulling on the brown wig. It felt like overkill. It felt like being extra. But putting it on made her feel better. Plus, it was what she was wearing when she checked in. It was important not to draw attention to herself. With the wig, if the attendant sees her, he won't know what she really looks like.

Then Mia opened her door and saw the familiar grill of a supercharged truck. Her heart caught in her throat, her breath getting caught up in her windpipe, and she couldn't stop her eyes from tracking upward.

There was Alex, pretending to look somewhere else.

Hands shaking, Mia turned and started walking toward the office. Almost as if on instinct, she started limping, hoping the difference in gait would deter him.

She passed the office slowly, noting the half-asleep clerk gazing dazedly out into the parking lot. Would they call the police for her if she called for help? A quick glance around the motel told her no—this was not the kind of place that wanted the police around.

She forced herself to stay calm, not to break into a run once she got around the corner. He could be right behind her. She kept her head bent forward.

That was hours ago. Now, Mia warily passes some of the little cash she has left over the counter at a bus stop. She's exhausted. The run-in with Alex made her sick with anxiety, but now that's quieted to a dull thrum.

As she climbs aboard the bus, holding out her ticket for the driver, she chews on her lip, mulling over her options. What's her plan?

First, she knows she needs to get out of the city. As far away as she can. It was obvious Alex had a tracker on something of hers—now, all she has is the key to the Camaro, her phone, and a little cash. Her phone is powered off, and she's not sure if she'll turn it on again for a while. It's too risky.

Mia thinks about the jewelry box and cash back in her hotel room. With it, she was set for a few weeks, at least. Without it, she doesn't know where she'll be sleeping tonight.

She had taken all her clothes off in the restroom at the bus stop, shaking them out. They couldn't be tracked, right? And even if they could, what reason would Alex have to plant a tracking device in his own clothes? That didn't make sense.

Mia stares out the window, kicking herself for not thinking of that. She should have taken his bag—he may not have planted a tracker in his own bag. The thought of it, of him rummaging around in the closet, planting a tracking device in her bag while she was out, talking to his mom or asleep, makes her sick.

This has been going on for a long time. And Alex had a contingency plan in case she ran. It's like being in a chess match you didn't realize had already started.

Mia tries to picture the pieces on the board. Has Alex realized he missed her yet? How long does she have before he catches on? She thinks of the Camaro sitting in the parking lot outside the motel. Will he realize it belongs to her dad and put the pieces together?

At the next bus station, Mia gets off and goes into the bathroom, wishing she'd brought her toothbrush with her. After cleaning up the best she can, she runs her fingers through the wig and boards a different bus. She tries to hide her face from the cameras she can see on the wall.

Would Alex have access to those? Mia's not sure. Alex is now an unknown variable in her life. She hadn't thought he was capable of everything he's done. It's impossible to know where he reaches his limits in finding her.

Mia slumps in her seat and draws her knees into her chest. She's so tired, yet every time she starts to drift off, she forces herself awake. She can't fall asleep, or the next thing she knows, Alex will be tapping her on the shoulder, forcing her to get off the bus, and throwing her into the backseat of his truck.

Mia's under no illusion that someone would help her. She thinks about the data on human trafficking. She thinks about how many women are abducted every year with no trace of them. People don't like to get involved in other people's lives, no matter what they say. Especially strangers' lives.

Her fingers itch, and she wishes she had her laptop. If only she could find some datasets, she could solve this problem. If she ran the numbers enough, she could better understand her odds of getting away from Alex and seeing her family again.

As she fights to stay awake, the landscape opens up around her. She stares out at the sky as the bus rumbles over Lake Pontchartrain. The sun is just dipping below the horizon, casting the sky in brilliant shades of orange. Mia wishes she could appreciate it more, but right now, her life is at stake.

The Water oaks and American elder trees fade away, replaced by empty ditches. Slowly, the long, straight highway starts to sprout ramps, and buildings show up on either side of the road. Mia watches, her heart growing tight.

Her stomach rumbles as they pass fast-food restaurants, their tall signs lit up against the darkening sky. The bus rounds a curve, and as if out of nowhere, New Orleans, with the Caesars Superdome and Hancock Center, comes into view.

It's her first time in the city. It should be exciting, but all she can think about is what happens when the bus stops, and she has to get off. With Lake Pontchartrain to the north and the bayou to the south, it feels like there's nowhere for her to run. She's at the end of the line.

She gets off at the Canal Street Station and looks around. It feels like the moment when a person steps out of a movie theater like reality is suddenly the strangest thing to fathom. Mia sees the Bernardo de Gálvez memorial, passes a Four Seasons hotel, then turns and realizes how she's going to make back the money she lost.

Chapter 17

Big City, Little Cash - Mia

The Harrah's Casino sign glitters in the reflection of the New Orleans lights. Mia takes a deep breath and then walks inside. The oxygen they pump in through the vents immediately wakes her up.

She finds the first public restroom and ducks in, grabbing a stall and sitting down. She fishes in her bra, pulling out what cash she has left. Counting it doesn't take long. After the bus tickets, she has just $145 left. Her heart races. It's definitely not enough for a hotel in this area, and it will only buy her a motel room for a day or two. She needs to make more money.

Mia considers finding a hostel, but they're usually full and prioritize international guests. She stares at the cash in her hand, wondering what her dad would do. Her dad would confront Alex, but that's not an option for her. She's not stronger than him. She has no footing in a fight against him.

She thinks about what Sara would do—probably go to the authorities. But Mia doesn't know if that's a good idea. With her recent theft charge, Alex could have easily fabricated a story about her stealing from him and then going on the run. In that case, if she goes to the authorities, they'll just arrest her and deposit her right back into Alex's waiting hands.

She worries her bottom lip, trying to think back to who she was before all this started. She was smart and dedicated. She thinks of being under her car, stubbornly planning to fix the tire, even if it meant certain death. She thinks about being the only one on the team to solve a complicated data problem.

What would that Mia do?

Outside the restroom, she can hear the faint jingles and ringing of gambling machines on the main floor. Gambling is statistically a very bad bet. The highest jackpot in recorded history is millions of dollars—but Mia knows that she's more likely to lose her money than to make it back.

She pulls $75 from her stash and tucks the rest away in her bra before flushing, washing her hands, and leaving the bathroom.

As she walks, she glances at the seafood restaurant and steakhouse on either side of her. Her stomach rumbles. She hasn't eaten anything all day, but she can't afford anything. She reaches into her pocket and rubs the bills between her fingers. Her mouth is watering at the idea of a steak and some steamed vegetables. Real food. She makes a promise to herself that the next time she gets the chance to sit down and eat real food, she'll stay in the moment and savor every bite.

The machines light up and the people wandering around, their eyes lit up in the purple and white lights, reminds Mia of the one and only time she'd ever been to a casino.

After turning 21, she went on a weekend trip with her parents and Sara. They hit up all the casinos in Montgomery. Mia's mom and Sara had goofed around the whole time, preferring to play a few slot machines and then head back to the hotel, lounging by the pool and drinking.

But Mia and her dad—they'd done rounds on the gambling floor, her dad explaining each game, which was fun, which were profitable, and how to win at each.

Having just earned her degree, Mia was fresh into her data analyst career, but she'd always had a mind for numbers and patterns. While they were standing there, it was like her brain latched on to the games, analyzing them. Understanding them.

Blackjack was the best game, relying less on luck than the others and more on numbers. In her job, Mia spent hours assessing figures and analyzing risk. The casino was a big risk, but she quickly started to learn how to minimize it.

And they started to win big. Too big.

"Mia," her dad had said after she made a couple hundred more. "Are you counting cards?"

"What does that mean?"

Her dad explained it to her, and she felt her face pale.

"Is that bad? Is it illegal?" she asked, her hand inching up to her throat nervously.

"No," he laughed, "it's not illegal, but casinos really don't like that."

"What will they do?"

"Kick us out, probably."

Eventually, a casino rep came over and asked them to leave, implying not too gently that Mia was not welcome back.

As soon as she got home, she'd done research on casinos. She fell into a rabbit hole researching basic strategy for blackjack and realized she'd been following it intuitively. The odds came easily to her. After that, she learned how to count cards even more effectively and less obviously, but she and her dad never got the chance to gamble again once her mom got sick.

Thinking about that birthday trip—how her mom and Sara had giggled relentlessly when Mia's dad told them Mia had gotten them kicked out—makes her feel sick. She realizes she'll never get that back, and her mom is only going to get worse. The grief hits her like it always does. Like a truck.

Her mind wanders to Sara, and she thinks, for just a moment, about calling her friend. Telling her about her situation. Sara would do anything to help her—and that's the problem. Sara would put her life on the line for Mia, which means a lot more now that she's pregnant. There's no way Mia is going to sacrifice Sara's well-being.

Mia will just have to figure out how to get out of the situation herself.

On the Harrah's gambling floor, it's a sea of flashing lights and pushy gimmicks to pull gamblers in. Mia stops, staring at the slot machines, watching the few people there, pulling levers and tapping screens.

Mia won't waste her money on slot machines. She purses her lips while looking them over—it's like they're designed for babies. Loud, brightly lit, and flashy, they draw in the people who have no idea what they're doing. People who just need to waste some time before dinner. She moves on, finding the roulette wheel.

True odds on a roulette wheel are too low. Mia walks right by the craps table, not bothering to look twice. In a moment of clarity, as she recalls the odds and calculates her potential winnings, she realizes it feels like her brain is back in her body.

The brain fog from the past few weeks is gone, and it's all because she's gained some space from Alex. How can one person affect her so much?

A dealer calls out to her, but she shakes her head, moving on. There's only one game in the casino that has the odds she's looking for, and she owes it to her dad to win some money on it.

Chapter 18

The Data Analyst - Mia

Having made her decision, Mia goes to the cage and trades in her cash for chips. Luckily, she must look old enough because they don't ask to see her I.D.

"Hi," she says, wandering up to the blackjack table shyly. "What game is this?"

"It's called blackjack," the dealer says. "Two-to-three odds."

Mia wrinkles her brow, like she's not sure what it means, then slowly sits down at the table. It brings back the first time for her, and she makes a show of listening to the rules of the game like she's never heard them before.

There are a bunch of other people at the table playing with her, and some of them give her advice she doesn't follow. Many of them have no idea what they're talking about, and when she bets against what they say, she just pretends not to understand.

The casino will figure her out soon enough, but she wants to delay that as long as possible. Acting clueless may help with that. She wonders, distantly, if that casino in Montgomery has a picture of her so they can make sure she doesn't return. Hopefully, the casinos don't share a database of card counters.

In an hour, she has doubled the original $75. She goes to the cage and cashes in half of her chips for cash, then returns to the blackjack table, waving around her arms like she's gained a newfound confidence from random luck. She treats herself to a drink and snack, then giggles at the person next to her like she's already drunk.

"I like this game," she says, twirling her hair around her finger. "I just keep winning!"

The guy gestures to his buddy as if saying, can you believe this girl? But the look slips off his face an hour later when Mia's winnings are piling up.

Split. Hit. Dealer bust.

Hit, hit. She takes the chips.

Double. She takes the chips.

Bust. She loses.

"You should play insurance on those," the man next to her says, leaning so close she can smell the Miller Lite on his breath. She makes an effort not to wrinkle her nose.

"I already have insurance," she giggles, "in case I crash my car."

She feels ridiculous pretending to be drunk, but she wants her consistent winnings to look like dumb luck. Mia continues playing the part of the silly, drunk girl while using basic strategy and counting cards to increase her winnings.

Four hours later, she has nearly a thousand dollars. The dealer is eyeing her warily, but she makes sure to stumble off her barstool, getting a nearby guy to catch her in his arms.

"Whoops," she says, "thanks for catching me."

"You might want to slow down a little," he says.

"Will do," she replies.

As soon as his hands are off her, she continues her stumbling out of the casino. If they think she might be counting cards and have someone tailing her, they'll be even more pissed when they see she isn't spending any money in the casino.

Smart people are profit-killers.

Deciding to treat herself yet again, Mia stumbles her way into the steak house, ordering a steak and salad. True to her word, she takes her time and chews every delicious, juicy piece of steak slowly. It's the best steak she has ever tasted in her life. Well, almost. Mia thinks about her dad and how much he loves to BBQ. She misses him a lot. By the time she's finished, she imagines she can pretend to sober up a bit. She takes her earnings and leaves the casino.

Outside, the balmy New Orleans air sticks to her skin. She may have more cash— but she still only has the clothes on her back, this brown wig, which is starting to get really itchy, and her phone, which she's still too scared to turn on.

She takes a deep breath and starts in a random direction. She passes several high-class hotels and wishes she could stay at one of them, but she knows she needs to hold on to as much cash as possible.

At a newsstand, she purchases a map of the city and sits down on a bench, processing the information. A moment later, she's outside a corner store, where she's able to buy a pack of cotton underwear, a pre-made travel hygiene kit, a frozen meal, another bag of beef jerky, and a small bottle of detergent.

After a long moment of deliberation, she decides to buy a cheap pair of jean shorts and an "I ♥ New Orleans" T-shirt. She's still wearing Alex's sweatpants and T-shirt, which she is thankful he didn't recognize. Besides being too big for her, they're also too hot in the New Orleans weather.

She winces as she passes over two twenty-dollar bills to the clerk, but she hopes that if she can be careful and go to different casinos, in a week's time, she may have enough money to get another bus ticket and make a long-term plan.

Cameras stare at her from every corner. Mia tilts her face away from them.

She just needs time to get herself together before deciding what to do. Once she's settled, she'll call her dad. And Sara.

After taking the wrong bus for 40 minutes, Mia gets on the correct route and steps off outside a cheap motel. She passes over more of her money—this time using Sara's name instead of Blanche's—and takes the keys. The motel clerk barely looked at her. It's one benefit of cheap hotels: they don't really care who stays there as long as they pay.

Her motel room is worse than she thought, with cigarette holes in the duvet and dust built up in the corners, but she's not on the street, and Alex doesn't have her.

She microwaves her meal and snacks on some beef jerky while she waits. The food stinks up the hotel room, but she doesn't care. It's nothing like the delicious steak she ate only a few hours ago, and she's surprised she's even hungry, but with being on the run, her stomach never feels full. After eating, she strips her clothes and takes a long, hot shower, double-shampooing her hair. There's even a razor in the hygiene kit that she uses to shave her legs and armpits.

When she steps out of the shower, she feels better.

Even being on the run, looking over her shoulder, and nearly running into Alex at the other hotel, she feels better than she has in months. She feels in control. She feels alive. She feels confident she'll make it out alive.

Mia stands in her towel and washes her clothes, including the new shorts and gimmicky shirt, in the sink with the laundry detergent. When they're about as clean as she can get them, she hangs them up from the shower curtain rod to dry overnight.

Mia pulls the duvet cover off the bed, pinched between her thumb and two fingers. There's no way she's letting that touch her clean body. Choosing the spot on the bed that looks least grimy, Mia crawls under the sheet and stretches out.

Her body aches from sitting on the bus for so long, and her fingers are itching to get back to blackjack, but she feels somewhat content as she falls asleep, thinking about how much money she might make the next day if she plays her cards right.

Chapter 19

Playing the Odds - Mia

Mia wakes up early, feeling well-rested. She brushes her teeth, braids her hair, and puts on her new outfit. She neatly folds the sweatpants and tucks them into the plastic bag with her detergent and hygiene pack.

Pulling out her map of the city, she locates the nearest library. It will give her a chance to do some research and get out of the motel. Before leaving the motel room, she glances out the window, looking up and down the sidewalk as far as she can.

No sign of Alex or his truck.

She steps out of the motel room, heading to the front office. Inside, to her surprise, is a dinky coffee maker and a few pastries. Seeing a line of ants snaking through the pastry case, she passes on the food but risks it for the coffee. It's hot and strong, and she hopes the fact that it's boiled means she won't get too sick if there's something wrong with it.

Spending a little more on the bus, she heads to the nearest library, where she's able to borrow a computer for an hour. She spends the time trying to find information about Alex and his mother.

Alex Bartlett, she searches. It turns up his profile at the mechanic's shop. A clipping from a high school football game. She keeps looking.

Alex Bartlett, crime.

Gone Mia: Deadly Deception

Alex Bartlett, stalking.

Alex and Blanche Bartlett.

Blanche and Alex Bartlett.

Blanche Bartlett and Alex Bartlett, Alabama.

This turns up a filing at a local courthouse's website. It takes Mia a little while to navigate because the website is more than twenty years old, but she manages to download the file and eagerly reads through it.

JOSEPH R. BARTLETT VS. BLANCHE K. BARTLETT
COURT DECREE – DISSOLUTION OF MARRIAGE

Mia's eyes scan through the document and read child in middle, child support, dismissal of a no-contact order.

Mia already knew Blanche had gotten a divorce, so this isn't helpful information. If she could read the documents from the case and learn more about what exactly happened, she might be able to gain the upper hand over Alex and his mother.

She wishes Sara were here with her—she might actually be able to decipher these documents. Under each filing in the case, there are comments, one attributed to J. Bartlett and one to B. Bartlett.

There are two documents linked, but the website leads Mia to a site with directions for requesting affidavits. She's about to give up and close the browser down altogether when she sees another option for a document preview. With her heart racing, she clicks, and an affidavit from the case opens up in front of her.

Comments from Joseph R. Bartlett in the case of J. Bartlett vs. B Barlett.

Mia leans forward so she can read the tiny font. It starts with Joseph clearly indicating that he doesn't believe their marriage is beneficial for them or their child, Alex.

...not only does the respondent, B. Bartlett, seem to harbor animosity toward our child, but she frequently uses him as a weapon toward me. This behavior includes sending A. Bartlett away to summer camp without consulting me and feigning ignorance when I question the whereabouts of my son.

There's a note that B. Bartlett refutes those claims. Mia reads on.

Additionally, B. Bartlett engages in emotionally abusive and manipulative behavior with both myself and A. Bartlett, including altering medications, limiting food, and creating an extremely toxic environment. When A. Bartlett returned from school with a poor grade, B. Bartlett first physically assaulted him and then did not allow him to eat an evening meal or breakfast the next morning. B. Bartlett has also engaged in stalking behavior, such as following me to work and lingering outside my offices...

Mia is about to click to the next page when someone taps her on the shoulder.

"Hey, hon," a librarian says, her glasses sliding down her nose. "Your time is just about up. I wanted to let you know you have about five minutes left. If you need more time, you can always come back tomorrow."

Mia thanks her and quickly prints as much information as she can from the court website. Then, she prints a list of casinos in the city before the computer automatically times her out.

She still has some time to kill before the casinos open, so she wanders down Bourbon Street, which is just as rowdy in the morning. She marvels at the committed travelers, already sitting at the bars, knocking back drinks, and it's not even noon yet.

Thinking back to the information in the divorce filings, Mia wonders how Blanche managed to get custody of Alex following the divorce if Joseph was so insistent on her being a bad mother. Mia wishes she had more time to read the other affidavits.

She turns the corner and sees the evidence of drunken debauchery lining the streets on either side—overfilled trash cans, empty bottles, and discarded accessories, like headbands, bracelets, and even a full pair of pantyhose. She doesn't have to walk much further, before she comes across two girls, one with her head bent over, the other holding her ponytail, and rubbing her back. The girl who is not being sick gives Mia a shy smile as if she's apologizing for her friend. Mia smiles back.

It feels good to wander around, going wherever she wants. She realizes Alex has had her on a very tight leash over the course of the past few months. She's stepping over a few glass bottles when she notices something else glinting in the sunlight—a pocketknife.

Mia stares at it for a long moment, trying to decide if she should pick it up. Then, slowly, as though someone might jump out from a doorway and yell at her, she carefully picks it up, noting that it's sticky with beer.

Someone must have dropped it the night before. She turns it over in her hands, looking for initials, but there's nothing. If they've even noticed it's gone, she doubts they'll come back for it.

She doesn't want to be the kind of person who carries a weapon for protection, but she can't deny that it might be nice to have. Even if she doesn't end up seeing Alex again, there are plenty of creeps in the city who might need to be deterred.

Mia's stomach begins to growl the moment she notices a bakery. The sweet smell of pastries has her mouth-watering. She treats herself to a beignet and savors the taste as she walks towards the bus stop. Before boarding the bus, she goes into a park bathroom and rinses off the pocketknife before folding it again and sticking it in her bra. It's half an hour of walking and more than that on the bus, but she arrives in front of Treasure Chest Casino just after it opens. She takes a deep breath and heads inside.

So that she's not carrying around a plastic bag; she finds lockers and pays to stash her things inside before heading to the gambling floor. This time, she gives herself $100 to play at the table.

The day doesn't start off strong—Mia is just unlucky, which, statistically, can happen. She just has to stay the course and keep her betting low, knowing better than to chase her losses. Three hours later, she's only just made her money back.

It's not based on math but on intuition. She pulls back from the table and decides to try again the next day. At least nobody can accuse her of card-counting with this losing streak.

Mia spends more money at the casino restaurant, savoring the fresh food. Then instead of leaving she decides to return to a different blackjack table. This time, she's actually winning, and she decides to call it a night before people get suspicious. With a few more hundred dollars to her name, she gets her bag from the locker and walks outside.

The sun is setting, and the sky is a dark violet. Around her, people are singing and partying, swaying drunkenly, their nights only getting started. Mia has to keep from rolling her eyes—gambling while drunk is, statistically, a very bad idea. She knows ninty-nine percent of these people will lose every cent if they walk into a casino.

She's two steps from the bus station when she realizes something is wrong, but it's too late. A strong arm wraps around her torso, pulling her back.

"Surprise," Alex says, like a boyfriend happy to see his girlfriend, giving her a hug, and before Mia can fight him, he puts a hand over her mouth, claps a handcuff on her left hand, and shoves her into the passenger seat of his truck, slapping the other end of the cuff to the bottom of the seat.

Everything Mia knows about abductions rushes through her head all at once, making it hard to think. Most people are abducted by someone they know. Most people abducted are teenagers or children. Abductors threaten their victims with weapons but never comply. If they're going to use it, it's better for it to happen in public.

Those kidnapped for ransom usually make it out alive. Those kidnapped in crimes of passion don't, especially when taken to a second location.

Her brain seems to reboot at this last thought, and she screams as Alex is shutting the door in her face. It's too late. She yanks on her wrist, the metal digging in painfully as Alex rounds the front of the truck, coming to the driver's seat.

As soon as he opens the door, Mia leans over, screaming out the opening.

"Help!" she screams before he gets in, shoving her over hard. Her head bounces against the other door, immediately giving her a headache. She feels the soft trickle of blood down the side of her face.

"Shut up," he snaps. One person across the parking lot turns to look in their direction, and Mia tries to yell again, to panic in their line of sight, but Alex reaches over, shoving her down with little effort. Alex keeps one arm on her, and with the handcuff holding her down, she's pinned to the seat. She starts to cry, the tears dripping onto the leather seat.

He backs the truck out of the parking lot and pulls away, leaving everything behind. In the side mirror, Mia can see her plastic bag, stuffed with over a thousand dollars, plopped on the sidewalk where she dropped it.

A few minutes later, they're on the highway and handcuffed, Mia can't get at Alex or grab the wheel. She's stuck, her escape retreating quickly in the rearview mirror. Her thoughts of being with her dad, mom, and Sara are gone.

Chapter 20

Back in my Possession - Alex

"What do you mean, she got away?"

Not knowing what else to do, Alex called Dave as soon as he got back in his truck. He sat there staring at the motel door, nearly cracked in half and hanging off its hinges.

Alex could peel out of the parking lot and drive up and down the street, looking for her, but before all that did was waste his time. And she left hours ago, so it was even more unlikely that he would find her, especially since she was onto him.

"I followed her to the motel, but when I got here, all her shit was in the room. She took off without it."

The line was silent for a moment, and Alex took a sip of his coffee—now cold—angrily. How much time was he going to have to waste going after her?

"I mean," Dave said, "wasn't the point of this to get your stuff back? If she left everything in the motel room, whatever she took from you should be there, too, right? I get wanting to press charges, but chasing her around like this isn't cool, man."

Alex clenched his teeth to hold back a groan—he'd messed up. Thinking quickly, he said, "It's just...she's got my mom's wedding ring. I searched the entire motel room, and it wasn't there. It's like she's keeping it just to mess with me. Mom's really messed up about it. You know how she is."

Dave did know how Blanche was. The guy was enamored with Alex's mom for some reason. Alex thought it had something to do with mommy issues and hated it, but Blanche was constantly inviting Dave over for dinner so she could revel in the attention.

"That is rough," Dave agreed, sounding like he was mulling it over.

"Yeah, family heirloom," Alex lied. "Got it from her great-great-grandmother. It's one-of-a-kind. Emerald."

Dave let out a whistle through his teeth, and Alex heard clacking in the background—good, hopefully, Dave was figuring out what he should do next.

"Okay, man," Dave said, letting out a breath. "I'm going to help you with this, but after, I'm done, alright? I'm risking my license over this shit. But I'm trusting you. Just get your mom's ring back, alright?"

"Yeah, for sure, man," Alex said, reaching forward to turn on the truck and back out of the motel parking lot. He threw his phone in the cupholder and started to drive somewhere he could get some coffee while Dave spoke.

"There are cameras everywhere," Dave said, his voice coming staticky from the cupholder. "We live in a real surveillance state. Which we can use to our advantage when we're trying to find someone. Which way do you think she went?"

"I have no clue."

"Can you hazard a guess?"

Alex leaned his head back against the seat, staring up at the fabric on the roof of his truck. If he was Mia, where would he go? He knew that she and her dad were huge Braves fans, so maybe it would make sense to go there. To a city she was more familiar with.

But, no—Mia was smarter than that. She wouldn't go somewhere that was obviously tied to her. So, what else did that leave?

"New Orleans," Alex said, knowing it was no better than a guess but not having any other ideas.

"Okay," Dave said, "send me another picture of her. I'll get back to you."

And ten hours later, he did. There, sent directly to Alex's phone, was a grainy video that clearly showed Mia in her brown wig, walking through a casino. Alex could hardly believe his luck. He called Dave right away.

"Hey, man," Alex said, "thanks again for this."

"Yeah," Dave said, "but like I said, this is it for me. You just make sure your mom gets her ring back, and don't do anything stupid."

Dave found the exact casino by looking at the logo in the background, and Alex had driven into the city, getting a hotel downtown. In the video, it showed Mia playing blackjack, which made sense to Alex. She had a brain for numbers. He wondered just how much she'd won over the last few days. She must have been counting cards—how long did she think she would get away with that?

Seeing her again for the first time, walking out of the casino, Alex felt his heart pick up with anticipation. It was the same feeling he got when he used to go hunting with his dad—back before the divorce. That pounding heart, finger on the trigger, eye through the sights feeling, waiting to see if it hit, knowing that the deer never even saw it coming.

Mia was fiddling with something in a plastic bag on her arm and didn't even bother to look up. For being so smart, she sure forgot to stay aware of her surroundings. After losing him and leaving the bug behind in that motel, she probably thought she'd really gotten away from him. That was a big mistake.

Now, Mia whimpers in the passenger seat, tears streaming down her cheeks. Alex is conflicted—on one hand, there's a part of him that actually feels tender toward her. When she lost her job, and he'd seen how devastating that was for her, he'd genuinely felt bad. On the other hand, he's trying to listen to a radio show, and her little noises are distracting.

"Shut up," he says, glancing over at her. "You lost. Just accept it and move on."

She stares at him, her eyes wide and disbelieving, and he feels a cool rage settle into his chest. He knows what she's thinking—that he's crazy. That no sane person would follow her like he did. But Alex knows the truth. The truth is that Mia thought she was smarter than him, thought she could get away without him tracking her down, and she was wrong.

In this world, there are the hunters, and there are the prey. And every person gets to choose who they are. When Mia decided to run, she made her choice. Running is what prey does. If she had wanted to, she could have taken him head-on, not started this wild goose chase. But she did. And he was a good enough hunter to find her, even without the GPS tracker. Yes, he had Dave, but he was the one who was smart enough to call Dave and come up with the story about his mother's emerald ring.

People can go on and on about rights, respect, and equality as much as they want, but Alex isn't stupid. What it truly comes down to is who has the power, and the reason Mia is handcuffed in his truck right now is because he has the power. He outsmarted her.

After a while, she goes quiet, and when he glances over, she's gone limp, her chest rising and falling steadily, her arm bent at an awkward angle to accommodate the handcuff. Alex chuckles to himself—this is exactly what he's talking about. A hunter would never fall asleep in a situation like this, but prey, it's almost like they're asking to fail.

Chapter 21

No Help - Mia

Mia decides that her best chance for escape is to feign being asleep. Closing her eyes is also a reprieve from the fact that, despite her best efforts, she's right back where she started before she took her dad's car and left Alex behind.

Except that's not true—she's not right back where she started. Her situation is worse now because Alex—and his mother—know that she knows about their plan. Mia was in danger before, but now they've recognized her as a threat, which means she's in a lot more danger.

Her heart races. She doesn't know where Alex is taking her or the full extent of their plan, but she knows that her window of opportunity for getting away is closing quickly.

After Alex shoved her into the passenger seat, he'd groped around her body, eventually finding her phone in her back pocket. She still hadn't turned it on out of fear that he would find her, and now she wishes she had just used it since Alex managed to track her down anyway.

Part of her wants to ask him how he found her, but another part of her wants nothing to do with him and would rather have to keep wondering than hear his pompous, annoying voice.

Here, in his truck, she wonders how she ever found him attractive. Looks can be so deceiving.

She thinks again of that moment he grabbed her outside the truck stop, and a deep-seated irrational fear comes to her, hard and fast, almost making her dizzy with its intensity.

What if he planted a tracker in her?

Would that be possible? She tries to remember the past few months, and if there had been any time that she was so out of it, Alex could have implanted a tracker in her arm without her knowing. But her memory is so fuzzy she can hardly remember anything at all, except for the fact that she lost her job and moved. Big events stick out, but it's like all the smaller memories that usually make up the day-to-day are gone.

Her stomach roils at the thought of a foreign object in her body, and she has to take deep, steadying breaths to keep the nausea at bay, and to convince Alex that she's sleeping.

Then, suddenly, she feels the truck rolling to a stop. Her brain jumps into overdrive, trying to figure out what she should do.

Slowly, she opens her eyes, pretending like she's coming out of a deep sleep. When she sees Alex, she forces herself to smile sleepily, pretending that in the moment, she's forgotten everything.

"Alex," she says softly, her voice thankfully rough and low because of the screaming. It adds to the sleepy effect. "I have to use the bathroom."

He has his hand on the door handle and stares at her for a long moment. She can see a fuel pump just past him. They're at a gas station in the middle of nowhere, with huge, empty fields extending on all sides away from the stop. Faintly, she can hear bugs and birds through the windows on the truck, and her body aches to be outside again.

Alex is still handsome—Mia has to admit that, but the difference is she doesn't find him attractive. There's a big difference, one she never understood before.

She remembers, suddenly, the thought she had that first night on the side of the road. That he was handsome, and statistically, most serial killers are. It's how they get their victims to trust them. If only she hadn't been stranded that day. She was at the wrong place, at the wrong time, and now she's trying to figure out if she'll get away from this man at a gas station.

"You can wait," he says, finally, his fingers tightening on the door handle like he's going to get out of the truck. Panic pulses through her. She makes a show of shifting uncomfortably and making a face.

"The baby—" she says, "it's pressing on my bladder. I have to pee so bad."

None of that is true, of course. If she were pregnant, which she's not, according to the pregnancy tests, the baby definitely wouldn't be big enough inside her yet to press on her organs, but Mia is banking on Alex not knowing that. She's hoping he'll just blindly believe what she says, not caring enough to learn about pregnancy since he'll never have to experience it.

"I'm not stupid, Mia," Alex spits. "This is just a dumb ploy for you to try and get away from me. So just shut your damn mouth and sit back in your seat. Listen to me, Mia—if you try anything while we're here, life is going to be a lot worse for you back at home. Just be grateful that I came to get you before you ended up homeless on the streets of New Orleans."

Then, apparently fueled by his little speech, he reaches over and tears the brown wig off her head like he's tired of looking at it. He slams the truck door, and Mia watches as he shoves the wig into the trash can by the pump.

Her heart is writhing in her chest, beating erratically. This is her one chance to get away. How can she get Alex to let her out of this truck?

The idea comes to her, and her cheeks pre-emptively flush with the humiliation of it. But it's the only plan she can think of, and she's running out of time.

Mia closes her eyes, leans back in her seat, and imagines she's just entered a bathroom. She imagines that she's sitting on the toilet, about to use it.

She hears the click of the gas pump, indicating the gas tank is full. If she can't do this now, she's done. She takes a deep breath, trying to get her body relaxed. It feels like the time she had to have a drug test done to volunteer at a youth center—when you're trying to go, it's impossible.

Mia hears Alex grunt just outside the driver's side door, and suddenly, a wave of fear pushes through her, and that's enough.

She pees her pants.

Mia puts her hands to her cheeks, almost wanting to laugh at the ridiculous situation. A grown woman, forced to incontinence. Then a tiny sob lodges in the back of her throat when she realizes how terrifying this situation is if it's come to that.

She uses that sob and pushes it until she's crying again, gasping with hysterics, right as Alex opens the truck door.

"Oh—what the—" he says, his eyes darting from her face to the huge wet spot on her legs and the truck seat. "Oh—" he says, putting his hand over his mouth, gagging a bit before he slams the truck door shut and stalks around to the other side. For a moment, right when he rips the passenger side door open, Mia thinks he's going to hit her, but he just jams the key into the handcuff and undoes it.

"Go," he says, his hand still pressed to his mouth. Mia climbs out of the truck on shaky legs. He's just going to let her go into the gas station?

Then he closes the truck door and follows behind her. When they walk inside, Alex grabs a pair of sweatpants featuring an American flag print and hastily buys them before shoving them in Mia's direction. He follows one step behind her to the bathroom, instructing her to throw her shorts away.

While in the bathroom, Mia looks around, her heart deflating when she realizes there's no window. For a moment, she stands on the toilet, reaching her hands toward the ceiling tiles, but as soon as she pushes one to the side, a mound of dust and a dead spider fall on her, and she abandons that idea.

What works in the movies isn't going to work here. She wishes she had her phone.

Alex pounds his fist on the door, and she turns, quickly flushing the toilet so it sounds like she's been doing something in the bathroom other than planning her escape. Stripping, she wipes her legs down with wet paper towels and soap, then grimaces as she has to pull the sweatpants on with no underwear. They're stiff and scratchy, but she supposes they're better than sitting in soiled pants.

She's had less than five minutes of privacy in the bathroom before she has to open the door and see Alex's face again. He still looks angry and disgusted, and he grabs her by the bicep, pulling her out of the bathroom and walking them back to the front of the store.

Other than the clerk, who looks mostly bored and is absorbed in a magazine, there's nobody else in the building. Mia's chest constricts when Alex purposefully positions himself so he's walking between her and the cashier, so Mia would have to try and push past him to get the cashier's attention.

And then what? Would he even believe her? Would Alex rip her away, make up some sort of story? Mia's heart pounds. The person behind the counter is a man, which makes her feel like he'll be more inclined to believe Alex, especially since the clerk saw Mia walk in here with soiled pants, and now she's leaving in a cheap pair of gas station sweats.

The moment passes, and Alex is shoving Mia back out into the sunshine. Alex pulls a can of Lysol from the bag and opens the passenger seat, spraying it liberally.

He's so preoccupied with his effort to clean the seat that he doesn't see the blue Cadillac pull up on the other side of the pump. Mia's body starts to shake with anticipation when she sees a woman in the passenger seat—someone who might help her. The man in the Cadillac puts the gas pump in and then heads inside the building.

Deciding she has no time to waste, Mia lurches around the front of the truck, yelling.

"Hey!" she says, waving her arms. It takes her longer than she thinks to get around the front of the truck, and then she's around the fuel pump, just entering the woman's line of vision.

She looks older and actually reminds Mia a lot of Blanche. From the car, the well-pressed shirt, and the pearls around the woman's neck, Mia can tell she's upper-class, and the woman actually clutches her purse to her chest when she sees Mia running full speed and shouting.

"Help—" Mia starts to say, her eyes connecting with the woman's just as Alex's hand closes around her bicep. He yanks her back so forcefully that her neck blossoms with pain, and she gets an instant headache. She stumbles, twisting her ankle, just before another burst of unbelievable pain rockets through her cheekbone, making it feel like her brain bounced around in her skull.

She holds a hand to her face, blinking in shock.

Alex hit her.

Mia's gaze meets with the older woman's again. The woman in the Cadillac looks away as Alex drags Mia back around to the truck, this time shoving her into the tiny backseat and handcuffing both her hands around a headrest.

She screams and writhes and tries to meet the lady's eyes again, but she's looking down at her purse determinately as Mia wails at her, her breath fogging up the back window.

Chapter 22

Backbone - Mia

They've been driving for at least three hours before Alex speaks again.

Mia's entire body hurts. Her head is pounding from the shock of Alex's fist against her face. Her cheekbone throbs and she's pretty sure the skin split open, leaving a tiny trail of dried blood down her cheek that she can't wipe away. Her neck stings from the force of being whipped back, her legs are sweating and chafed from the cheap sweatpants, and, on top of everything else, her stomach is still roiling.

"Do you want to know how I found you?" he asks, his voice quietly victorious. Mia wants to say no—to tell him that she doesn't want to hear a single thing coming out of his mouth, but the truth is that she does. The truth is that Mia will always accept information. It's always better to know as much as you can.

But it doesn't matter what Mia's answer is because Alex keeps talking.

"Remember when I found you on the side of the road? The start of our love story. Well, if you remember going to the diner after, you'll think of Dave."

Mia swallows, her throat dry and her saliva thick. Alex is saying this to her like it's not one of the first things she thought of when she realized she had to leave—the fact that Alex had a private investigator friend. Mia had hoped that Dave might have a sense of morals and wouldn't help Alex go after his victim, but Mia was wrong.

"Well, Dave is really good at finding people. I knew when you left, Mia. I set everything up on purpose. Do you think I would let you figure out my plan? You thought you were being a good little spy?"

Mia's stomach clenches, remembering her dash out of the apartment and how she'd rushed to get everything ready. How she'd felt with her ear against the door of Blanche's apartment, hearing what they were saying about her.

Had they known she was there?

But then, why hadn't Alex caught her until New Orleans? Why let her get her dad's car? Why do any of that?

"I wanted to play a little cat and mouse with you," Alex says, rolling his shoulders as though he can read Mia's mind. "I knew you would run. I wanted to show you that no matter where you go, no matter how far you get from me, I will find you. And I will bring you home. Always."

Mia feels another tear slip down her cheek, and she hates herself for it. Logically, she knows that what Alex is saying isn't true—more than likely, he just got lucky in finding her this time. If she could get out of the country, his chances of locating her would go way down, but then she'd be even further away from her parents and Sara. Plus, she couldn't live on the run. What kind of life would that be?

But knowing and feeling were different, and at Alex's words, Mia feels trapped. Isolated. Alone. She tries to swallow again and coughs instead, the tremors wracking her body.

"You better not throw up in this truck," Alex snaps. "Pissing yourself was more than enough."

Mia feels humiliated and turns to stare out the window. There must be a way out of this. There has to be. She leans her head against the glass.

***

Blanche is waiting for them when they return to the apartment, literally clutching the pearls around her neck. Mia thinks of that other woman—the one at the gas station who had the chance to save her—and feels a brand-new wave of fury push through her.

Alex has her by the arm, leading her into the room, and Blanche turns. Now, knowing what she does, the woman seems less grandmotherly, and more like an evil witch. She's wearing a pale blue dress and matching pumps, her hair perfectly styled. Mia thinks of her time in the shitty motels, washing her clothes by hand and finger-combing her hair, and wants to dump a bucket of water on Blanche's head. Mia wonders if this is how Cinderella felt when she met her evil stepmother for the first time.

"Where has she been?" Blanche asks, not even bothering to look at Mia. Mia bristles at this—she's only been back for a few minutes, and she's already in the process of disappearing again.

"New Orleans," Alex says, putting a hand on Mia's back and pushing her further into the room.

"And how did she get to New Orleans?" Blanche asks, her voice a pitch higher than usual. With more clarity, Mia is already noticing all the ugly things about this woman—her nasal voice, the way she stands, and how shaky and wrinkly her hands are, despite Blanche constantly trying to defy her age. Mia wants to laugh and cry at the same time. Laugh at Blanche's lame attempt at vanity, and cry because right now Blanche has the control.

Suddenly, Mia longs for her mother, and Mia has to work hard to keep a sob from rising out of her—even if she manages to get out of this situation, her mother is lost to her.

But her dad isn't. Sara isn't. After being on the road and getting away from Alex for that short while, Mia sees that the world is so much bigger than this small town and the people in it. There's a whole life of possibilities, and for the first time, Mia thinks her circle might be too small. She needs more than her elderly dad and a friend who lives towns away.

Something like this wouldn't have happened to her if she had a group of friends all checking on her when she fell off the map. And she probably wouldn't have been so easily swayed by Alex's handsome looks and charm.

"I—" Alex starts, his eyes darting over to Mia, and she realizes he doesn't know about her dad's car. Alex doesn't know that she took the Camaro first, then the bus. That means he's exaggerating his ability to find her. Mia rolls her lips into her mouth, wondering if Alex truly did just get lucky when he found her at that casino.

"Did you hit her?" Blanche asks, finally looking at Mia and apparently just now seeing the bruise and blood trailing down her cheek. To her surprise, Blanche actually sounds upset about this.

"I had to," Alex says, though Mia would argue that he didn't. He could have gotten her back in that truck without his fist hitting just under her eye, but Mia thinks he was waiting for the chance. After he'd done it, and she had been blinking through stinging tears, she'd seen a look of satisfaction. It made her think of a previous boyfriend who had always been a little too rough with her, but she'd left him before he could actually cross the line and hit her. In that moment, she made a promise to herself that she would never be with a guy who mistreated her again...but now here she is with a man who actually hit her. She starts to blame herself. How could I let this happen?

Then, Blanche walks toward Mia, and she's brought back to the moment. She tries to take a step back, but Alex is there at her back, holding her in place. Blanche leans in, peering at the cut, her face screwed up.

"Really got her good," Blanche murmurs, reaching out like she might try to touch Mia's cheek. Mia jerks back away from her, horrified that she might want to touch the open wound on her face. Blanche's face sours, and she looks up at Alex again.

"How did she get to New Orleans? How did she have money for a bus ticket?"

Mia feels Alex stiffen behind her, and she presses her lips together to avoid smiling. She likes knowing that he isn't as smart as he thinks he is. She knows that he doesn't know how she got to New Orleans, and the longer it takes him to answer, the angrier Blanche looks. There's a long moment of silence.

"Never mind," Blanche snaps, waving her hand in Alex's direction. Mia can see that gesture in Alex. It's easy to picture how growing up with a mom like Blanche might have made him the way he is. For the briefest moment, she starts to feel sorry for him, and then she remembers the throbbing in her face and pain in her neck, and the feeling dissipates. Feeling sorry for Alex is the last thing she needs to feel. She needs to keep her wits about her, and figure out a plan for getting out of there.

"Mom—" Alex starts, but she looks fiercely at him, and he stops talking. Mia wishes she had that power.

"What do you know about what happened, Alex? Or have you just been bumbling around like an idiot, like usual?"

Mia starts inching toward the door, but Alex reaches out and grabs her, hauling her further into the room. She wrenches her arm from his grip, backing away from both of them, spit flying from her mouth as she yells.

"You're both insane," she says, looking between the two of them, who look genuinely shocked that she's saying anything at all. "I'm leaving."

"The hell you are," Alex says, easily catching her and pulling her back when she tries to make for the door.

"You can't keep me a prisoner," Mia says, feeling feral as she twists in Alex's arms. He can hold her easily, but she won't stop trying. Blanche looks at her with an equal measure of annoyance and amusement. "I will keep trying to escape. I will never let my guard down again," something comes to Mia, and she debates it, then decides the situation is already so far gone that it can't hurt, "I'll kill you in your sleep! I swear, I will make sure you never feel safe again."

Blanche's expression darkens, and she turns to Mia, looking genuinely scary.

"Alex," Blanche says, "put her down."

Alex hesitates, then complies. Mia urges her feet to run for the door, but she feels caught in Blanche's gaze like it's a beam from an alien spaceship.

"Why did you leave?" Blanche asks, tilting her head slightly.

Despite herself, Mia hears her own voice, answering, "I heard you two talking. About me." She hates how the tears well in her eyes, "And how you were the one sending me those hate messages. You made me feel crazy."

"We're all a little crazy, Mia," Blanche says, glancing at Alex. The second her eyes look away, Mia tries to bolt for the door again, but Alex drags her back once more. Blanche fetches a chair from the kitchen, and they force her down into it, tying her hands and feet down with some Gorilla tape.

"If you scream," Blanche says, "I'll wrap this Gorilla tape around your head, do you understand me? I don't want to have to ruin that pretty hair, but I will if you can't behave yourself."

"Go ahead," Alex mutters as he flops down in a chair. He's breathing heavily, and Mia feels a bit of pride that she's at least been able to wear him out. "She'll just wear a wig."

Blanche laughs at that, and then the two of them leave the room. Mia hears their muffled whispers a moment later, and her body trembles. She tries to twist her wrist to loosen the tape, but she's stuck. She wonders if she's ever going to leave his apartment again.

Chapter 23

Home Truths - Mia

Mia watches as Alex slams out the front door, and Blanche follows behind him, locking it and putting the key in her pocket before turning back to the room. With all the modern amenities in this building, they decided to keep ancient doors with manual locks. Mia stares at the lock on the door, wishing it was a modern bolt instead.

Blanche looks at her, and disappears from the room, and then returns with a wad of gauze, a large bandage, and some other materials from a first aid kit. Mia rears back when Blanche sits down in front of her, but Blanche just tuts and shakes her head.

"I'm not going to hurt you, dear," Blanche mutters, her eyes skipping up to the wound on Mia's face. "That son of mine is a real piece of work."

"Would you call this entire situation not hurting me?" Mia asks, surprised at herself. Here she is, tied to a chair, at the mercy of this woman, and she's standing up to her.

Blanche raises one perfectly groomed eyebrow.

"Not physically, no," she says, leaning forward with an alcohol pad. It stings, but Mia holds still. The last thing she needs is an infection. As Blanche works on the cut, she keeps talking. "I didn't want any physical harm to come to you."

"Whatever you say," Mia says. "Just so you know, it was physically painful when you were leaving me those hate messages. Depression is a physical thing."

Blanche shakes her head. She's so close that Mia can smell her perfume, strong and floral. It makes Mia want to sneeze. It's so obvious that Blanche is always trying so hard to remain beautiful, but just like her son, there is nothing attractive about her. Looks can only carry a person so far before what they're really made of shines through, and if that's ugly the whole package is ugly. Blanche and Alex might look attractive at first glance, but Mia knows the truth.

"You know, Mia," Blanche says, her voice deceptively gentle. "I was actually in an abusive relationship. I know these days everyone wants to say you can hurt someone without touching them—I don't think that's true. I think if someone doesn't lay a hand on you, it's up to you whether or not you get hurt. But my ex-husband—"

—Joseph, Mia thinks—

"—he was abusive. The real kind of abuse. He threw me around when he was mad. Would hold me down, push me. Once, he grabbed me by the hair."

Mia thinks about this, remembering the affidavit she read from Joseph's point of view. Without being there, it's impossible to know who's telling the truth. Based on the fact that Blanche is the one who currently has Mia tied up and held prisoner, Mia is partial to Joseph being truthful about Blanche's abusive behaviors, but why would Blanche feel the need to make up this story. It's not like they're girlfriends sharing secrets.

Plus, Mia also thinks about how Blanche looked when she saw the bruise on Mia's face. Maybe there is some trauma there for her. In a divorce, Mia supposes, there doesn't have to be a bad guy. It can just be two terrible people going their separate ways and pointing fingers at one another as they do.

"You're talking about Alex's dad," Mia whispers, thinking that if she can keep Blanche talking, she might be able to get the older woman on her side. If she can pretend to care, pretend to be her friend, maybe it will work in her favor.

"Yes," Blanche snarls. "I suppose it was ultimately my fault for having such bad taste in men. That man ruined everything—Alex's childhood and our futures."

"How did he ruin your future?" Mia asks in a soft voice, wincing when Blanche presses a little too hard on her wound.

"Because—" she stops, glancing at Mia like it's a trick question. Then, Blanche glances at the door as if she expects Alex back any second.

When Blanche stands up quickly, wringing her hands together, Mia feels a little tremor of fear run through her body. Blanche is becoming more agitated, and Mia can't get away. She was really hoping for the opposite, she was hoping to gain her trust.

"Because," Blanche says, pacing back and forth in the room, her hands fluttering in front of her like little birds. "He stopped paying my alimony. That's the money I earned by staying with him as long as I did. How am I supposed to live? I never developed any skills because I was too busy keeping house and cooking for him. What's my career supposed to be as a woman approaching sixty?" Is there a crack in Blanche's voice? Is she going to cry? Mia doesn't think the woman is capable of shedding tears.

Mia swallows, watching as Blanche stalks across the room, where she comes to a stop in front of her red Gucci purse. From her spot in the chair, Mia can see an envelope sticking up from the top of the bag, and when Blanche sees her looking, she quickly tucks the envelope back into the bag, giving Mia a dirty look. Mia's heart sinks. Any hope she had of befriending Blanche is gone.

"The entire system is rigged," Blanche says, rolling her eyes and spinning on her heel, pacing back toward Mia. "Women always get the short end of the stick— custody of the kids without the money to pay for it. Nothing for the emotional damage. Men just take and take and take. Even when Alex was a kid, he was learning how to do it himself. When he was going to vocational school, he met this skank of a woman and had the gall to bring her into my house. On Thanksgiving! I'd worked all day to prepare a meal, and now, suddenly, another mouth to feed in front of me. Well, how was I supposed to know she was allergic to peanuts?"

Mia's eyes widen as she takes in Blanche's flustered appearance, the manic look in her eyes. What happened to this girl?

"I always fry my turkey in peanut oil," Blanche continues, "every single year. Alex knew that. Not my fault he brought her home and told her to eat up. Not my fault her EpiPen was buried at the bottom of her bag. All the screaming and yelling at me to find the damn thing!"

Mia is horrified. What happened to the Thanksgiving guest?

Blanche seems to realize she's working herself up and stops, running her hands over her hair to smooth it down. She takes a deep breath. She's not a woman that likes to lose control.

Mia presses her lips together, trying to forget the image of what Blanche is describing. Did she purposefully delay getting that girl her EpiPen? What happened to her?

"But what does that have to do with me?" Mia asks, wriggling her hands and feet. She feels something brush against her finger, and when she looks down, she sees a little sliver of the tape brushing against her hand. She snaps her gaze back up to Blanche, hoping she didn't see. She might be lucky; Blanche has shifted and is looking at her image in the hall mirror.

Mia moves her fingers again, grasping the loose sliver and pulling as best she can with just two fingers. It tweaks her wrist painfully, but she keeps tugging at it, hoping it'll come loose. She's not sure what she'll do next, but it's a start.

"I saw your dad parading around town," Blanche says, finally. "Months ago. I was just leaving my lawyer, who told me there was nothing I could do about the alimony case. It was devastating. Then I walk out and see Mr. Agostino, driving around in his nice car, paying for his friends' lunch."

Blanche laughs to herself, tugging on the silk scarf around her neck.

"At first, I thought to myself—maybe I could get that man. Maybe he'd be interested in a woman with some class. But I tried, and he turned me down. To stay with someone who can't even use the bathroom on her own."

"You shut your mouth," Mia says, her body jolting but contained by the tape. She snarls at Blanche, who just laughs. Her entire body revolts against the idea of Blanche flirting with her father. Mia's not at all surprised that her dad turned Blanche down—he's a faithful man, and besides, he's always had a penchant for identifying the bad apples. It's part of what made him so successful in business.

"That's fine. I guess I'd be upset, too, if my mother lost her mind. But it only took a little bit of research to figure out who you were, honey. The internet makes everything far too easy. I found your father and thousands of pictures of you. From high school and college, I even found your address! Your house was in the background of one of your pictures—Mia, you think you'd be smarter about cyber-safety."

Mia's body goes cold at the image of Blanche in front of her ancient computer, clicking through pictures of Mia's family.

"This is all for nothing," Mia says, laughing with a surprising intensity when she realizes what Blanche is saying. "You get that, right? When my mom got sick, my dad had to liquidate almost all of their assets to pay for her treatment. He cashed out their retirement funds, sold all their investment properties—and emptied everything except my college fund to pay for highly specialized and experimental treatments. There's basically nothing left. I might get their house, but he has my blessing to sell that, too. We've been doing everything in our power to get my mother back."

"I don't believe you," Blanche says, turning and throwing her scarf over her shoulder, which infuriates Mia. "If he was selling everything, why still be driving around in a Cadillac? Why buy lunch for a table of six people?"

Mia stares at Blanche—whose hands are shaking. Blanche's eyes are darting around the room, her mouth constantly moving.

Her dad drives around in the Cadillac because it's fully paid off and has hardly any miles on it. He and his friends alternate paying for each others' lunches. But

Blanche seems to be convinced that Mia and her family have far more money than they do.

Another thought comes to her—and it hits her like a truck. Mia feels her vision blur as she realizes that Alex finding her on the side of the road, trying to change her tire, wasn't a wrong-place-wrong-time situation. He sabotaged her vehicle. He targeted her.

If what Blanche is saying is true, the entire thing was a setup from the start. Alex wasn't a random bad apple that Mia had the bad luck of meeting—he was a weapon sent in by his mother.

That day, on the side of the road, what would have happened if Mia had said no to the date at the diner? What would have happened if she had turned Alex down and just gone home? Would he have followed her?

If her car had problems again after the tire and Alex happened to show up, she would have been suspicious. Would he have "run into" her at the grocery store? And if she'd kept saying no?

Her blood runs cold at all the memories of Alex in her bed, cuddling her. She thinks of him walking into the bathroom, opening the curtain, and grinning as he watched her shower. At the time, she'd thought it was cute. Now, looking back at all those instances, they seem creepy.

"So, what?" Mia says, cocking her head. "Are you going to place a ransom call?"

Blanche laughs, putting her hand to her heart.

"Heavens, no," she says, laughing. "That's criminal activity. We just need you, and Alex married. We've already gotten most of your money, but once your parents pass away, we'll have the inheritance."

"And what about me?" Mia asks, her voice coming in gasps. "You'll take my inheritance—if I even get anything—then what? Are you going to kill me?"

Blanche shrugs, turning and holding up the end of her scarf, running the fringe over her fingers.

"This is insane," Mia says. "You're not going to get away with this."

"We'll see," Blanche says, giving her an infuriating smile.

Chapter 24:

A Melody of a Fight - Mia

Blanche continues talking, pacing back and forth in front of Mia.

Mia's fingers are cramping, but she keeps grasping for the loose piece of the tape, pulling on it harder and harder each time. Finally, it starts to loosen enough that she can start to rotate her wrist within the tape. Even with one hand free, she might be able to overpower Blanche.

She looks at the older woman, wondering if she could get her while dragging the chair around with her. What is she capable of?

"And the price of bleu cheese!" Blanche is saying. "You wouldn't believe it."

Mia coughs when the tape pops off her wrist, hoping it covers the sound, and Blanche looks at her sharply. Mia's body lurches forward, almost as if acting on its own, as she lunges toward Blanche, catching her off guard.

Somehow, though Mia has the element of surprise on her side and is a good forty years younger, Blanche is able to get her hands on Mia's side, giving her a hard shove, which sends her tumbling to the side, her body hitting the floor with a thud, her contained wrist and ankle screaming in pain.

Something metallic falls and hits the floor beside Mia's head.

Blanche runs out of the room, and Mia can hear her phone dialing.

"Alex, you need to get back here—"

155

Mia tears her attention away from Blanche and to the matter at hand. If she moves quickly, she might be able to get out of the chair and get to the door before Alex gets home. This time, she's going straight to a police station. She doesn't care if Alex has woven some story about her and the things she's done—she'll be happier locked up in a cell than here, on the floor of Alex's apartment, fighting for her life.

Her eyes drift up to the glinting metal object that's fallen beside her head, and she realizes with a start that it's the pocketknife she found on the ground in New Orleans. With her free hand, she reaches up and grabs it.

Once her other hand is free, she's able to brace on the wall and right herself, bending at the waist to see through the tape on her ankles. The tape is thick and strong, and the knife struggles to get through. Mia can feel the blood pulsing in her ears as she works.

She knicks her thumb and the inside of her ankle with the knife but doesn't feel any pain. There's too much adrenaline coursing through her body for that.

When Mia finally gets the tape free, she lets out a little sound of triumph, and she stumbles to her feet, her legs and knees stiff from more than an hour of being held in the same position.

Blanche comes running back into the room, and when she sees Mia holding the knife, her face goes white.

Mia adjusts the grip of the knife in her hand. Will she use it if she has to? She takes a step toward Blanche, who retreats a step into the kitchen. Beyond the kitchen, there's just the bathroom. Otherwise, there's nowhere for Blanche to hide.

As if they have the same thought at once, Blanche turns and runs toward the bathroom, but Mia is faster, skidding to a stop outside the bathroom and grabbing Blanche by the back of her cardigan, ripping and pulling her inward.

Blanche turns, hitting Mia hard across the face, making the wound that's already there burn with a new and very intense pain. Mia's eyes water and her mouth turns acrid. For a moment, she thinks she might be sick again.

The two of them land together on the linoleum kitchen floor, and Mia scrambles back from Blanche. Blanche groans, holding her left hip, but Mia stares at her, worried it's for show. Mia's holding the knife in front of her with two hands, which are shaking.

"Just give me the key," Mia says, her voice low. Everything inside her is fear right now—fear that Alex will come back, fear that Blanche might hurt her more, fear that she might have to use the knife if she wants to escape.

"No," Blanche says, a laugh still in her voice despite the change in situation. "You're going to have to use that knife if you want to get out of here."

Mia gets to her feet, watching Blanche, who's still gripping her hip and gritting her teeth. A moment passes in the kitchen with nothing but the sound of Blanche's groans filling the space.

Walking over to her, Mia stands over top of the older woman, thinking that if Blanche grabs her, she'll go after her with the knife. But when Mia reaches down to take the key, Blanche rolls over with sudden agility, grabbing Mia's legs and alligator-rolling her to the floor.

Mia hits the floor hard on her tailbone and cries out at the pain. The pocket knife hits the floor and skitters across the kitchen, sliding under a wall heater on the other side.

Blanche starts to crawl away from Mia, and when Mia reaches out to get her by the ankle, Blanche kicks back, catching Mia across the jaw. Mia curses loudly but gets a handful of Blanche's skirt. The older woman is losing her steam, and Mia is able to crawl over her, fighting against Blanche's hands to grope in her pockets for the key. Blanche's scarf comes off in the struggle, and Mia balls it in her hand.

When Mia's hand wraps around the key, and she feels the cool metal against her skin, she could cry. She falls back on her butt, wincing at the pain there, and scoots away from Blanche, who's trying to get up off the floor but struggling.

"Get back here," Blanche says, her voice strained. "Mia! Stay away from that door!"

Mia almost laughs at the futility of the command until she gets one foot away from the door, and it opens, revealing first the barrel of a black gun and then Alex behind it.

"You'd better sit back down," he says, his eyes flicking to Blanche on the floor behind them. At the sight of Alex, Blanche immediately starts gripping her hip again, crying in pain.

If Mia sits back down in the chair, she knows it'll be over. Especially now that Alex has a gun. Thinking quickly, she throws Blanche's scarf in Alex's face and turns, running back into the kitchen and kicking Blanche on her way in. His mother cries out, and Alex screams after Mia.

"You bitch!"

Mia crouches and, groping blindly, manages to get her hand on the pocket knife once more. She and Alex reach Blanche at the same time. Blanche has managed to sit up at this point, and Mia comes around behind her, grabbing her hair and pulling her head back.

"Ah," Blanche says, and Mia can feel the woman's body shaking with fear as Mia presses the pocketknife to her throat. Alex's eyes go wide, and the gun lowers slightly.

"Back. Off." Mia says, voice low. "You think I won't, Alex, but I will."

Alex's hand is shaking, making the barrel of the gun wobble. Mia stares into it like it's a black hole. Her entire universe reduces to a single, tiny point. If Alex shoots, she's done, but if he does, Mia will hurt Blanche.

Her hand trembles on the knife. Will she be able to do it? If she does, is she just as bad as them?

"Alex," Blanche says, sounding slightly choked. "Put that gun down."

Mia has an idea, and she looks into Alex's eyes, feeling the months she spent with him there and the lingering intimacy between them. She tries to picture what it was like from Alex's perspective, being intimate with a woman he was actively planning to harm. She has to swallow to keep the nausea at bay.

"Alex," Mia says, "do you know what your mother said to me the second you left the apartment?"

"No," Alex says, his eyes darting between Mia and his mother. "Shut up."

"She said you were a real piece of work. She said you were a waste of space. A means to an end."

"Close your whore mouth," Blanche says to me before directing her attention to Alex. "That's not true, baby. You know I'd never say that about you."

"She said she wishes she got an abortion."

Alex's eyes widen, and the gun dips slightly. Blanche tries to struggle in my arms, but Mia presses the knife closer to her neck, restricting her movement.

"Alex," Mia says, "remember Thanksgiving when you were in college? What happened?"

Alex's brow draws together, and he looks from Mia to his mother, confused.

"Melody," Alex says, voice soft. "She died. From the peanut oil."

"Yeah," Mia says, staring right at him. "Well, your mother could have gotten Melody her EpiPen. Remember? She was looking in the bag—but she was mad that you brought Melody home without telling her. So, she let her die."

"What?" Alex says, while at the same time, Blanche says, "She's lying!"

"She told me just now while you were gone!" Mia shouts over the top of both of them. "You could have gotten Melody her EpiPen but chose not to. Your mother is a sick person, Alex! She's using you! She's the reason—"

Mia's next words are cut off when an ear-splitting crack rips through the room, and she's suddenly covered in blood.

Chapter 25

911 - Alex

Alex watches, as if in slow motion, as the bullet travels through the air and lands in his mother's chest. She's looking at him, mouth open, and he's sure that if she weren't choking on her own blood, she would be calling him a worthless piece of shit.

He thinks of Melody. She was in his mechanics class with him and so, so smart. The other men in the class refused to pair up with her, but after Alex did the first time, he realized she finished her assignments in half the time, changing brakes and rotors and identifying engine problems in record time.

"I grew up in a garage," she'd said, shrugging and winking at him when he'd given her a stunned look. "If the rest of those jerks wanna be here the rest of the night.—let them, but not us. We're outta here."

Melody was gorgeous, with thick, wavy auburn hair and dark brown eyes. Alex started taking her to drive-in movies, the two of them sitting together in the bed of his truck.

She was also a child of divorce, and it was easier to talk to her about what it was like growing up. It was the worst in fifth grade.

His parents had recently gotten a divorce, and for some reason, his mom told Alex that he wasn't allowed to see his dad anymore.

Alex hadn't understood, because his dad was always good to him. They would go hunting and fishing together, and sometimes his dad would comment on "how nice the quiet was" while they walked through the woods together.

Those outings with his dad were always more peaceful and relaxing than those with his mother.

All at once, Alex realizes that his mother has been terrorizing people since Alex was a kid. His entire body aches for the childhood he never got to have with his dad, whom Blanche had managed to get a no-contact order against.

Instead, Alex's childhood had been full of Blanche—never after-school activities or hanging out with friends because she needed him home. He had no job to make his own money until he was eighteen, and she hadn't been happy with the idea of him going to Reid, either. His mother had wanted him at home, where he could wait on her hand and foot.

That is, until his dad stopped paying the alimony money, and Blanche suddenly needed cash to fund her lifestyle. Alex thinks of her closet, of the rows and rows of designer shoes, the real leather, the custom handbag shipped over from Italy that she'd picked out for her birthday.

At first, when his dad stopped paying, Alex thought that maybe he and his mother could sell some of her things, and as much as he didn't want to, she could move in with him. On his mechanic's salary, they could make it.

But Blanche didn't want to make it. She wanted to keep filling her apartment with useless designer crap, going out to eat at nice restaurants, and turning up her nose when the bill came, waiting for Alex to take it.

When Mia brought up Melody, Alex looked at his mother and knew the truth. He saw written all over his mother's face that she had been taking everything from him for years and would never stop.

He can't stop himself from seeing her—Melody, gasping for air on the kitchen floor while his mother fumbled with her bag. Her blonde hair fanned out around her face. Melody's calloused hands grasping at Alex, trying to gain purchase, to get another breath of air.

At first, Melody had gasped instructions, trying to claw her way to the bag.

"In the pocket!" she'd said, her voice rough. "At the top!"

Alex had never felt pure panic like he did in that moment, with Melody's head in his lap as he desperately dialed 911, his fingers shaking and hitting the wrong buttons.

Then, after a full thirty seconds of not finding the pen, Melody stopped talking altogether. Alex had dropped the phone the second the operator picked up, screaming the address and for them to come help. He'd walked across the kitchen, ripping Melody's bag from his mother's hands and turning it upside down, grabbing the EpiPen when it tumbled out.

But by the time he stuck it in Melody's thigh it was too late.

He'd always believed his mother was just panicking, unable to think straight like him.

Until now.

His body takes over, his brain comprehending what's just happened, and Alex drops the gun, running to his mother's body. He can't think, the incessant repeating of no, no, no, no, no, no, no, no, no, no, no cycling through his head, drowning everything out.

And then he starts to scream.

Vaguely, through the haze, he sees Mia start to stand, her legs shaking, her body slipping around in the blood as she tries to stabilize herself.

"Call 911!" Alex hears himself scream. The screaming feels like throwing up, like his body is exorcising a demon through his mouth. His mother is dying. His mother is dying right in front of him.

The image of Melody superimposes over his mother, and he rises up on his knees, bracing his arms, placing his hands on her heart, and trying to do CPR. Blanche is still choking, gurgling, her eyes bulging as she looks around the room like she just needs to find someone to blame for this.

He sees it again, the bullet traveling through the air. When he was standing there, holding the gun, it felt like his brain didn't belong to him. He looked between Mia and his mom, the knife against his mother's throat, the tears on Mia's cheeks.

His mother hardly looked scared, even with the knife to her neck.

He remembers the night it all came to a head when he'd finally decided to stand up to his mother months ago. He'd been coming home from a long day at the mechanic shop when he ran into the package handler at the front door.

"Hey, man," Alex said, and the package handler checked the name on the package. "Oh," Alex said, holding his hands out. "That's my mom. I can take it up to her."

The delivery guy tipped his head and turned, heading back to his truck. As Alex climbed the steps, he read the label on the package.

Louis Vuitton.

When he got to his mother's apartment and saw that nasty wedding soup boiling on the stove, he slammed the package down, startling her.

"What is this?" he'd asked, gesturing to the package. Blanche had gathered herself immediately, clutching her scarf to her chest.

"Those are some shoes, Alex, and very nice ones, so you don't need to go slamming them around."

"How are you affording this?" he'd asked, his eyes darting around the apartment. It didn't look like she'd sold anything.

"Oh," she'd said, waving her hand at him. "You know I'm just borrowing your credit card until I get back on my feet."

"Mom," Alex said, putting his hand down on the package as she tried to lift it. Yes, he had given her his credit card. For groceries. For medication. "I can't afford designer shoes every week! What happens when you max out that card, and we don't have a way to feed you?"

Blanche stared back at him, then her lip started to wobble, and he felt like an asshole. What kind of man slams into his mother's apartment and makes her cry? Right after she loses her alimony payment?

"I have an idea for a way to get some money, but I know you're not going to like it," she'd said, dabbing at her eyes with a handkerchief from her pocket.

"What?" he asked, but he already knew.

Another girl, of course. His mother had always had a pretty strong opinion on who he dated. It led him not to date at all after Melody until his mother started suggesting certain girls.

Girls who were lonely. Easy to isolate. Easy to drug and pilfer money from before dumping it at the last minute. After the last time, he'd told his mother in no certain terms that he wouldn't be doing it again. He wanted to find someone he could really be with.

"This woman," Blanche said, "her father parades his wealth all over town, so I feel like it would hardly matter to the family. We get her and get her parents' inheritance."

And Alex had agreed, sabotaging Mia's tire while she was inside the restaurant, having lunch with her parents. He'd come to her on the side of the road, and when he returned to his truck and saw her sitting there, head lolled back, asleep, he'd thought that maybe, this time, he could just run away with the girl. Get away from his mother once and for all.

But those thoughts only ever lingered in the back of his brain. They weren't permitted to come to the forefront.

Now, Blanche jerks under Alex's touch, and her eyes fly open for a moment. Though she's covered in blood, and he can barely look at her, he can read the look in her eyes as easy as ever. She'll haunt him in death just as she haunted him in life.

He keeps trying to do CPR, yelling for Mia to call 911. His hands are completely coated with blood. It's on his face, soaking his shirt and caked under his nails. He keeps pumping at his mom's chest, his arms growing tired from the effort.

Alex needs to save her, and he wants her to die. His brain feels like it might cleave clean in half.

Chapter 26

Victory - Mia

Mia can't move.

The blood is warm, liquid, dripping, covering her. She gasps, breaking her paralysis, when Alex rushes toward her, and she drops the pocketknife on the floor with a thud.

All around her is the scent of blood. Acrid, sharp, metallic. She tries to breathe through her nose and starts to feel like she's going to panic. Has she been hit? Her brain runs an inventory of her body as she moves her hands over her torso and face—no wound, but her hands are covered in blood and leave a sticky residue all over her face.

She gags, turning and throwing up on the linoleum just as Alex drops to his knees in front of Blanche, who's making a strange gurgling sound in her throat like she's drowning in herself.

With her entire body shaking, Mia uses the kitchen counter to get to her feet. Her hands slick against the wood, sliding out from under her a few times before she can gain a firm grip and get all the way to standing.

The picture unfolds in front of her: Blanche, flat on her back now, and Alex leaning over her, his hands on her chest. Through the pounding in her ears, Mia vaguely hears him breathing and grunting, his arms braced.

He's giving her CPR. Every time he presses down on her chest, more blood oozes out from Blanche's body. Mia is going to be sick again.

Then Alex looks up at her, tears in his eyes, his mouth wide open, and Mia realizes he's screaming at her, over and over: Call 911.

She jumps to action, her feet sliding in the blood that feels like it's coating the entire kitchen. Breathing hard, gagging a little in her throat, she runs into the living room with tiny, jittery steps, her phone reaching for Blanche's phone in her purse, where she had thrown it after calling Alex earlier.

Then, Mia pauses.

Blanche is on the floor in the kitchen, surrounded by blood, either dying or already dead. Mia should be calling 911 right now to get help for someone who needs it. It was her first instinct, but she can't stop picturing that look on Blanche's face when she was going on about Melody.

Mia can't shake the feeling that, given the opportunity, Blanche or Alex would have taken the opportunity to kill Mia if it would have made them a profit.

She can still hear Alex screaming and Blanche's labored breathing. It's like she's watching a choose-your-own horror movie.

Slowly, she walks to the bathroom and washes her shaking hands as calmly as she can. Then, she walks back into the living room and, using Blanche's scarf, opens the envelope in her purse that she was trying to hide earlier.

Mia's eyes widen, and she quickly puts the paper back in the envelope, before turning and walking into Alex's bedroom. She opens his desk drawer and places the envelope in the top, slightly open.

The screaming is getting louder. She can hear Alex calling her every obscenity in the book, alternating between asking her for help, calling her a bitch, and asking if she's calling 911. As if moving on autopilot, Mia walks back to Blanche's purse and picks up the phone, dialing 911 and placing the phone on the table, faintly hearing the sound of the operator on the other end.

Mia steps over the discarded gun and into the kitchen. She spots the key on the ground, only splattered with blood, and luckily not completely drenched like everything else. Mia holds the key tightly on her way back past Alex. Blanche has stopped making noise and is now lying limply on the kitchen floor, her face already startlingly pale.

Alex is on his knees in front of her. Mia is struck by how much he looks like a little kid at the moment. As she walks past, Alex raises his head numbly to look at her. The tiniest bit of life enters his body when he sees her moving toward the front door.

"Hey," he says, though Mia just keeps moving as though she can't hear him. "You can't leave!"

Mia keeps walking, one foot after the other, her gaze locked on the door. After unlocking it, she's stepping over the threshold when she hears Alex coming through the kitchen doorway.

Her legs feel like jelly, and her body is still bruised and aching, but she runs. She runs to the stairwell, down the steps, and to the front of the building, practically feeling Alex's breath on the back of her neck. When she glances behind herself, she sees he has the gun, and her heart drops.

After everything, he's still going to hurt her?

Mia swallows, tears blinding her when she realizes he has nothing to lose. Her feet fumble down the rest of the steps, and she leaps over the last two, her body slamming into the door at the front of the building, throwing it open, and bursting out into the sunshine.

"Mia!" Alex screams, his voice in pure, violent rage.

Mia runs faster than she ever has in her life. She thinks of her mother, her father, Sara, and all the people she'll get to see and meet when she survives this. She will survive this. She will not allow Alex to take one more thing from her.

"I won't shoot you if you stop, Mia!" Alex calls. A kid on a bicycle across the street screams, and their parent yanks them up, pulling them away and into their house.

When Mia rounds the corner, she sees bright blue and red lights, and a cruiser veers to the side of the road, two officers opening the doors and pointing their guns at Alex.

Mia doesn't stop running. If she does, Alex will get her.

"I said, get down on the ground!" the cops yell, and too late, Mia realizes they're talking to her, too. In an instant, she realizes that, of course, they don't know whether she has a gun too. She doesn't have a chance to stop as she gets closer to the cruiser, and the cop fires once, then twice, and her entire world goes black.

Chapter 27

The Envelope - Mia

Mia wakes up to the sound of rhythmic beeping. Instantly, she knows she's in the hospital, and she gasps, trying to sit up, but she's tangled in a thousand cords.

"Shh, shh," a nurse says, "don't worry, love, you're safe here."

When Mia manages to pry her eyes open, there's a handsome man peering down at her. Mia opens her mouth and screams at the top of her lungs, startling him so hard he nearly falls over backward.

After that, they only assign women to Mia's care team. The doctors explain to her that the bullet entered through her torso, cracking her bottom-most rib but otherwise leaving her unharmed. After they stopped the internal bleeding, her body was able to start healing.

But her brain wasn't.

"You went into a coma exactly one week ago," the doctor says. "Physically, there was no cause for it—you weren't bleeding, your vitals were good, you didn't have head trauma—but the body has a way of giving the brain what it needs. Considering the trauma you went through, it's not surprising that you fell into a coma."

"Where's Alex?" Mia asks as soon as she can speak again. The doctor cocks her head, lips pursing.

"Your dad has been here every day," she says, "who is Alex? Another family member?"

"Alex is in custody," a voice says, and Mia looks up to see her father standing there, just inside her hospital room, like he's not sure he should come in.

Every inch of her body hurts, but she bursts into tears, holding her arms up for him to come and give her a hug. The doctor excuses herself and warns Mia not to over-exert herself.

"Hey, honey," her dad says, settling into a chair by the bed.

"Dad," she says, her chest constricting with sobs. "I'm so sorry."

"Mia," he says, laughing a bit through his tears. "Given the circumstances, I don't think you really have anything to apologize for."

"I can't believe I let him trick me like that," Mia says, looking up at her dad with tears in her eyes. "I can't believe I was so stupid."

"Alex is a scumbag," her dad says firmly, shifting to cross his arms. "According to the lawyers, this is something he's done quite a few times. Well—with much tamer outcomes than what happened with you, but several women are coming forward, claiming he and his mother stole upwards of a hundred thousand dollars from different people."

Mia is quiet for a moment, her eyes focused on the stiff white blanket covering her in bed. She fiddles with a loose thread, then looks up at her dad, his face coming in warbly through the tears in her eyes.

"I won a thousand dollars playing blackjack," she says, trying to shrug like it's no big deal, but the pain makes her wince.

Her dad does laugh, however. Mia regales him with the tales of counting cards, pretending to be drunk, and hustling the casinos while she was in New Orleans. She's trying to keep her voice light, trying to avoid upsetting her dad too much, but the truth of the situation hangs over them like a heavy black-out curtain.

Visiting hours end at eight, and Mia grips her dad's hand, not wanting him to leave.

"I think you should move in with us for a while, Mia Bear," he says, his voice quiet. "Your mother really misses you."

Mia waits until her dad leaves, stopping and waving at the door, before she bursts into horrible, body-wrenching tears.

***

"Mia, hey, we should probably start to get ready."

Mia stirs, her hands brushing across unfamiliar pillowcases. When she opens her eyes, she sees Sara standing over her, bags under her eyes.

"Oh, hey, thanks," Mia says, "I'll just jump in the shower."

"Coffee?" Sara asks.

"Please," Mia mutters, and they share a grin.

Sara's baby, Benny, was born with a heart defect. It was temporarily serious, but he's since had surgery and his recovery is going well. The doctors are optimistic that it won't affect the rest of his development or his life.

But the stress of the surgery and attachment issues mean that Benny is up most of the night, screaming. When Mia wanted to be closer to the state's capitol for Alex's trial, and Sara was at her wit's end staying up with the baby every night, it worked for them both for Mia to stay in.

Mia helps with the cooking and cleaning and switches off with Sara at night to care for Benny. Lately, he's been sleeping a bit better, but the sleep deprivation is still intense.

Despite the long nights rocking a crying baby, Mia feels more like herself than she has in months. After her release from the hospital, she went to stay with her parents, but once her ribs healed, she had to have a hard conversation with her dad.

"I think," she'd said, sitting down to coffee with her dad, "that I've let my life stall. I'm not saying it's my fault what Alex did. I know that, but I just keep thinking that if I had a bigger social life and if I was living my life to its full potential, I would never have been a target for him in the first place."

Her dad had cried, but they'd both agreed that it was for the best.

Mia steps out of the shower, switches on the hair dryer, and grabs her brush. Immediately after everything happened, she'd had nightmares. She couldn't sleep at all. Every time she closed her eyes, she saw Blanche's limp body on the kitchen floor and the huge puddle of blood oozing out of her body.

Now, Mia shakes her head a little, running through the list of coping mechanisms the therapist gave her to combat those intrusive thoughts. First, she focuses on her hand on her hair, the feeling of the hot air blowing on her wet hair, and how it fans out across her neck softly. Grounding.

Then, she thinks about Benny, his sweet little face. How it feels when she's holding him as he falls asleep, his little hand wrapped around her finger.

Her heart rate slows, and she sets the hair dryer down, throwing a little product in before moving to the kitchen, where Sara has prepared toast and coffee for both of them. Mia sits at the table, and they eat quietly together.

Sara's mother arrives a few minutes later, hanging her coat and coming in, cooing over Benny, who is fast asleep in his crib. Sara taps her watch, and they quickly finish their breakfast, saying goodbye to Sara's mother and moving to the car.

They take Sara's minivan because Mia still hasn't picked a new car. Her dad is urging her to take the Camaro, but she's not sure if she wants it with all the bad memories. She enjoyed driving it and might look for a muscle car when she finally gets around to buying a new one.

The drive to the courthouse is fast, and on the way, Mia and Sara listen to the radio. The city passes by Mia's window, but she pays very close attention to the news.

"Today marks the final day of the Alex Bartlett case, in which local Alabaman man faces a first-degree homicide charge for the murder of his mother, Blanche Bartlett. Alex is also facing several other minor charges, including extortion, kidnapping, aggravated assault, and theft.

"What may have otherwise been a relatively low-key case has turned into a total media storm due to the reaction from women across the nation. It first started with Bartlett's previous victims coming forward to testify in the case and grew into a movement on social media that focuses on how difficult it is for women to go to the authorities when they experience domestic abuse.

"The turnout at the courthouse today is expected to exceed anything in Alabama's court history, based on the social media interest and outpouring of love and support for those affected by Bartlett's behavior.

"A pinnacle of today's proceedings will be the long-awaited testimony from Mia Agostini, a primary victim and witness in the murder of Blanche Bartlett and chief witness to several of Bartlett's assault charges. Agostini was hospitalized for several weeks due to the injuries inflicted by Bartlett and the subsequent interaction with local police.

"We'll all look forward to seeing how this case concludes, and we wish all those women outside the courthouse the best as they continue their movement."

The show runs an ad and Sara reaches over as they turn the corner, and the courthouse comes into view. Mia sucks in a sharp breath, bringing her hand to her mouth.

There are hundreds of women lined up outside the courthouse, holding various signs and posters. One reads BELIEVE WOMEN, and several of them have statistics about domestic abuse, which Mia respects and appreciates.

Sara pulls up to the secured entrance, and the guards ask for their information. Once they park, a guard escorts them inside the building. Across the lawn are counter-protesters with signs about men's rights. Mia ducks her head as a camera flashes.

Inside, the courtroom is quiet, muffling the sound of the women outside. For the past few weeks, Mia and Sara have come to court every day, watching the proceedings, Sara holding Mia's hand.

Today, Mia has her testimony folded in her pocket so she can read from it when it's her turn. The courtroom fills and fills with people until there are some standing in the aisles and along the back of the room.

Then they bring Alex in.

Only his hands are cuffed, and Mia remembers instantly the cuffs he used on her in his truck. She remembers the way the metal dug into her wrists, and she hopes he's feeling that now. She hopes he feels just as trapped as she did.

The judge calls the court to attention, and the prosecutor approaches the bench, whispering something. Alex's lawyer approaches the bench, and the entire courtroom shifts while waiting to see what they're talking about.

"The prosecution will enter into the case a new piece of evidence."

"Good morning, everyone," the prosecutor says, buttoning her suit jacket and standing before the jury. "I would like you all to direct your attention to the documents pictured on the screen here. At first glance, it's a little difficult to understand what these documents are, but I can translate them for you."

The prosecutor walks over to the board, gesturing to a bolded line in the center of the document.

"As you all know from previous testimony and evidence, Blanche Bartlett was engaging in theft to replace the funds she lost when her husband stopped paying alimony. As that was a sealed case, we previously could not use documents from that case in our arguments with you. But this document was found in Alex Bartlett's desk drawer, and as you can read here, this line reads, Sample was not a match."

Putting her hands together, the prosecutor walks back toward the judge.

"What sample, you may ask?" the prosecutor says. "Well, this is from BioLab Industries, a company that specializes in paternity tests, and this is a test requested from Joseph Bartlett, confirming that Alex Bartlett is not a DNA match to him. Blanche and Joseph were married in 1984, and Alex Barlett was not born until 1989. Because this proved Blanche had committed adultery during their marriage, Joseph Bartlett was released from his alimony requirements. This better explains Ms. Bartlett's need for money, but more importantly, it gives us a clear motive. Alex Bartlett found this document in his mother's things, and, upon realizing he'd been lied to about his paternity, decided to take his mother's life."

"Objection!" Alex's lawyer says, standing and gesturing. "That's speculation."

"Strike that from the record, jury, disregard the prosecution's last statement."

"I'm sorry, your honor," the prosecutor says, turning back to the jury. "What I mean to say is that it's my assumption that Alex found this document, and it contributed to his ill-intent toward his mother, ultimately resulting in her death."

On Alex's side of the courtroom, the lawyers are scrambling, clearly trying to figure out how they can refute this new piece of evidence. Mia stares at the back of Alex's head.

Alex's lawyer gets in front of the courtroom and argues that a piece of evidence introduced so late in the case can't be reliable. The jury doesn't look convinced, and neither does the judge.

"The prosecution calls Mia Agostini to the stand."

Mia takes a deep breath and walks to the front of the courtroom. Her hands are shaking, but she wears in and climbs to the stand. When she's seated, she can see everyone in the courtroom.

Including Alex.

He's sitting back in his chair, his hands clasped together, staring right at her. His facial hair has grown out a bit, and there's a bruise dusting over his left eye. It looks painful. Mia hopes there's more where that one came from.

"Mia Agostini is one of the most recent victims of Alex Bartlett, and she's here to testify today. Please consider her testimony."

Mia clears her throat and looks out into the courtroom, catching Sara's eyes. She gives her a sober nod.

"Good morning, everyone," Mia says, licking her lips. "Five months ago, I found myself stranded on the side of the road. A handsome stranger stopped to help me—except he wasn't a stranger. Alex Bartlett already knew me, and that's why he sabotaged my tire so I would get a flat. I could have lost control on that highway. I could have hit another vehicle or hurt another driver. What came next turned out to be even worse than that.

"For months, Alex drugged me with his mother's medication, keeping me subdued and emotionally unstable. He planted evidence on me that implicated me in theft. He tampered with my alarms, making me late for work until I was eventually let go. He poked and prodded at me until I completely changed for him. He isolated me from my friends and family.

"When I realized that I wasn't in a safe situation, I managed to escape from Alex and his mother and run to another state. But Alex found me and dragged me back to his apartment, where his mother was waiting. So far, everything you've seen in this case has shown you proof that Alex is a murderer. There's no doubt about that.

"But it's also worse than that. For months after Alex kidnapped, assaulted, and imprisoned me, I couldn't sleep through the night. I was afraid to go in public. To this day, I have no interest in dating, and I'm not sure that I ever will. What Alex took from me is more than just the months I lost in an unhappy and abusive relationship—it's the security I lost. The confidence in myself.

"Today, I ask that you not only consider the murder of Blanche Bartlett but also the events leading up to Alex pulling that trigger. It was the messy and traumatic climax to a story that never should have started in the first place. I ask that when you're considering the verdict," she says, to the jury, and then, "and the sentencing," to the judge, "that you consider what Alex will do when he has the opportunity to take advantage of, and abuse, more women. Blanche deserves justice, I deserve justice, and every woman on the street deserves to live her life without fear of men like Alex Bartlett. Thank you."

Sara refrains from cheering but holds a thumbs up to Mia, whose hands are still shaking when she climbs down from the witness stand. She's already been cross-examined by both lawyers about what happened that day, but today was about giving her the opportunity to say her peace.

Mia rejoins Sara in the seats, and Sara puts an arm around her, pulling her close for a moment. The proceedings drag on, and the jury leaves the room to deliberate.

From talking with some of the other women, Mia has heard horror stories about trials dragging on for weeks and even months because the jury can't decide, leaving the victims in limbo, hoping for a conviction that takes far too long to come.

But this jury doesn't take very long at all, filtering back into the courtroom after just an hour of deliberation. Everyone in the courtroom stands, and the jury declares Alex guilty on all counts. Sara has an arm around Mia's waist, providing more support as her body sags with relief.

"I can't believe it," Mia whispers when they watch the jailers take Alex out of the room. Other than on the media, Mia will never have to see him again. Her heart already feels a little lighter.

They leave the courthouse arm in arm, and while on their way back to Sara's place, Mia checks her email, putting a hand over her mouth when she sees an email in her inbox.

"What?" Sara asks, glancing over at her with a worried expression. Mia takes a deep breath through her hand, all the excitement of the day getting to her.

"I got in," she breathes, "I didn't want to tell you because I didn't think anywhere would accept me, but I applied to a couple of universities. I don't know—I was thinking I might go for finance—"

"That's a great idea!" Sara says, reaching over and pushing Mia's arm playfully. "Where did you get in?"

"University of Pennsylvania."

"No way!" Sara says, swerving the minivan a little when she looks at Mia for too long. Then, making a split-second decision, Sara throws her turn signal on, pulling the minivan back off the highway. "I'll tell my mom it'll be a little while. We're getting margaritas!"

Mia throws her head back and laughs, thinking of what it will be like to move to a new city, continue her education, and start building a life she's proud to be living.

Epilogue:

Justice - Alex

Alex arrives at the maximum-security prison early on a Thursday morning. He stares out the window on the bus as he's carted from the local county jail to his new home. The intake guard gives him a toothbrush and a tan jumpsuit, then leads him to a cell that he shares with a cellmate, who's currently on the open toilet and who makes aggressive eye contact with Alex as Alex tries to figure out which bed is his.

All throughout the trial, Alex couldn't stop thinking about Melody, first seeing her, then seeing his mother's dead body. It was a never-ending barrage of horrific images, but sleeping was worse because then he saw a replay of the moment he pulled the trigger and killed his mother. He saw a repeat of the moment the life left his mother's eyes, and he was kneeling on the floor, his hands coated with sticky, cold blood.

He saw Mia walking out the door of the apartment and felt that familiar panic— he hadn't even finished losing his mother yet, and already he had to try and figure out what to do about the situation. He would have to hide her body. He would have to hide Mia's, too. Alex would only ever need to kill one person to know it wasn't something he wanted to do again.

He'd picked the gun up and ran after Mia, but every time he had a chance to take the shot, his body froze, and he couldn't do it. That scene played over and over in his nightmares. It was more punishment than prison could ever be.

Alex survives the first meeting with his cellmate and follows the intake guard around, seeing the library—about six ancient books on a shelf—the communal showers, in which you get four minutes before getting out, and the cafeteria, where Alex sits, by himself, every day for his first week in prison.

He gets his assignment—cleaning the communal showers—and wonders if there's anyone he can ask to put money in his account so he can buy some deodorant and toothpaste. His roommate never talks to him, only grunts and nods, and the guy spends most of his time on the toilet, so Alex has started holding it until they go out of the cell. The idea of using the open-air toilet isn't all that appealing, anyway.

Alex spends his time reading one of the untouched books from the library, doing his job, or lying awake in bed at night, staring at the ceiling, listening to his roommate snore atrociously loud.

A week later, Alex is sitting alone, eating his lunch, when a huge, burly man approaches him.

"Hey," the guy says, and Alex looks up, a spoonful of unidentifiable mush frozen halfway between his plate and his mouth. It tastes worse than nothing, and it's still better than that damn wedding soup. "What are you in for?"

Alex wishes he had more time to prepare for prison culture. He thinks of Mia and what she would say right now. Something like 84% of prisoners are stinky, or something like that. Alex clears his throat.

"Homicide," he finally says, thinking that might deter anyone from trying to mess with him, though it doesn't make him feel tough. He thinks of how he wakes up every morning to damp cheeks from crying in the night and knows that murdering his mother was the most cowardly thing he ever did.

"Oh, shit," the prisoner in front of him says, swinging his legs over the bench and sitting down across from Alex. In an instant, he's surrounded on all sides by super-buff men who probably spend all day lifting weights. Alex feels his throat get right. "How'd you get a body?"

Alex stares at him for a long moment, then looks back down at his mush. Is it better to lie? To say it was a bar fight gone wrong? Alex decides it's best to be honest. These guys might discover what he did and be even angrier if they knew he'd lied to them.

"I killed my mom."

The table goes quiet, and one of the guys drops his fork onto his plate. Surely, someone else in the prison must be in here for killing their parents. It's a relatively normal crime, Alex thinks.

"You killed your mom?" one guy asks, his eyebrow shooting up. And then, a guy at the end of the table speaks.

"You that guy from the TV court case? You abused all those women?"

Every head at the table turns toward him, and suddenly, the mush in his throat turns to concrete. He tries to swallow, taking a drink of his lukewarm milk, and struggles to get everything down.

"I—uh," Alex says, clearing his throat and still coughing.

"I Icy, fucker," one of the guys says, the table rocking as he gets to his feet.

"Sit down, Smith!" a guard calls, but the guy keeps walking toward Alex, his eyes locked on him like a missile.

"Mandy is my fucking sister," the guy says, then grins as he grabs the front of Alex's jumpsuit, hauling him up. "I'm going to enjoy this."

Note: If you or anyone you know is a victim of domestic violence, call 1-800-799-7233 or text BEGIN to 88788.

ABOUT THE AUTHOR

Hey there, your author here; I'm a retired executive with a knack for turning life's absurdities into literary gold. Armed with a master's degree in business and a therapist's recommendation to spill my guts onto paper, I accidentally stumbled into a full-blown writing gig.

It is like finding out your new hobby is actually your calling...who knew? My pen knows no bounds, darting effortlessly from heartwarming anecdotes to spine-tingling thrillers.

You see, my life isn't your typical retirement tale. It started with noble intentions—to care for ailing parents—but quickly spiraled into a whirlwind of caregiving, pandemic pandemonium, and enough drama to make Netflix green with envy.

Yet, through it all, I maintained my sense of humor and love for seeing the world through different eyes.

My writing mirrors the eclectic tapestry of my experiences—some tales drawn from my own adventures, others plucked from the colorful characters in my orbit, and some cooked up from the depths of my imagination, which sometimes scares even me. You might even call it "unleashing the Kraken."

The only constant? My unpredictable genre-hopping is much like my ever-changing moods.

Now settled comfortably into my forever home, I spend my days at home, writing my thoughts in tales that traverse realms of Adventures, Thrillers, and Mysteries, sprinkled with a touch of Children's Books and a Romance or two.

As you know, writing takes time, and I have several novels in the works. Therefore, follow me as an author to hear when my next book(s) will be coming out.

When you think of me, you know I'm home by the lake, nursing my diet coke and regaling my loyal pups with my latest literary escapades.

With at least a couple of decades left in the game of life, I aim to spend the bulk of it keeping you entertained—because, let's face it, doing what you love is the best plan.

VISIT
http://pagesbythelake.com